Prologue

September 1908
Mary

MARY WAITED IN THE stuffy attic bedroom, nerves swarming in her chest like a cloud of mosquitos. Had she made the right decision?

Frank was going to be so angry with her. It wouldn't be long before he came for her. The church bells had wrung out the hour just a few minutes ago.

Five chimes had sounded.

They were supposed to have been married at four.

How long had everyone waited?

Were they searching for her now?

Mary's eyes drifted to the elaborate wedding dress hanging on a hook next to the door. She hadn't even been able to make herself pretend by putting the dress on.

She didn't have the heart left.

Mary hadn't heart for much of anything in the last year. Yesterday had made it one whole year since Wolfgang had gone missing after the cattle drive.

Without him, Mary's life had been boring and lonely. Moving to the city had only made it more so.

1

Her work at her uncle's sandwich counter was only so stimulating, and despite the throngs of people, Mary was isolated from all of them. She was too quiet, too used to life on the farm, and she didn't know what to do with herself once she was done with work for the day. Edie, her uncle's housekeeper, wouldn't let her help with the chores outside baking the occasional loaf of bread.

To keep herself from languishing into a ghost in the attic apartment in her uncle's house, Mary had taken to teaching herself German in the evenings. Her uncle told her it was counterproductive. That she was better off learning Dutch, since that was their heritage, or French or Spanish—any language that didn't mire her in her grief. It was the reason he'd said he wanted to sell Wolfgang's banjo as well. He'd wanted to put Mary's dead husband's prize instrument in the window in his store and sell it--—and no doubt keep the profit for himself.

Her uncle wasn't a bad man. He'd taken Mary in when she'd lost everything. Her parents. Her husband. He was helping her sell the farms she couldn't manage on her own, but he was also a greedy man. If he saw an avenue to line his pockets, Uncle Levi would take it.

Mary had told him if he sold Wolf's banjo, she'd shear her hair off like she was a sheep.

Her uncle had let it be after that. He liked having Mary working in his sandwich shop because men would come in to buy lunch every day just for a chance to see her beautiful face and admire her golden hair.

If her uncle had his way, Mary would work at the sandwich counter forever. He didn't care that Mary was restless and unhappy. He'd also been annoyed when Frank had announced their engagement over the summer. Not because Mary was still grieving the loss of her first husband, but because if his niece were to wed again, she'd no longer be available for him to use to attract the town's young men in for lunch.

How many times had she and Frank met in this very room over the summer, just under her uncle's nose? It had been the perfect clandestine meeting space. Frank had rented the room when he'd first moved to town. He knew just how to slip into the house and up the back staircase without being noticed. And he had been the perfect way for Mary to forget that her whole body ached for missing what she could not regain. It was the only reason she'd agreed to see Frank, because she'd needed the distraction of physical pleasure to keep from drowning.

But then he'd begun pushing for marriage, and Frank's touch was no longer an escape.

She should marry him. She'd known that after she'd given herself to him that first time. It was what the rules of society demanded, and if anyone found out what they'd been up to, she would be forced into it. Mary knew all of that, which was probably why she had agreed. As much as she'd told herself taking another man to bed had been her first step in admitting that Wolf was gone, it had only been a coping mechanism.

The larger the wedding loomed, the more she felt like marrying someone else was too much of a betrayal for how much she still loved her husband.

Mary had pretended all day that she planned to arrive at the church in plenty of time. She'd sent her uncle on ahead of her, and he hadn't hesitated. With the house empty, Mary had ascended the stairs to the large attic bedroom, taken off her everyday dress and stared at the immaculate dress Lettie had created where it hung on the wall.

The very core of her soul had recoiled from it. She'd been lying on the bed in her underthings ever since.

Frank would no doubt find her here soon. She wasn't sure what would come next, but she wasn't looking forward to explaining why she couldn't marry him.

Not after everything.

Mary stood to open the window next to the bed. The stuffy late summer heat threatened to suffocate her. She was growing more anxious the longer she waited. The sooner this was over with, the sooner Mary could move on from this awkward pause in her life.

As Mary settled back on the bed, in only her undergarments, and positioned herself in the path of the breeze, she began to count. When she reached two hundred twenty-two she finally heard footsteps on the stairs.

She sat up on the bed, wanting to appear at least conscious of the humiliation she'd just put him through.

The doorknob turned, and the door creaked open. That was unusual. Normally, Frank burst through like he was going to explode if he didn't make love to her immediately.

"Frank?" she asked, sitting up and pulling a quilt across her chest.

A figure darkened the doorway, but through the shadow of the unlit staircase, Mary could not discern a form.

Fear replaced any anxiety she'd been feeling, and Mary fought light-headedness as she crept toward the door, clutching the quilt to her like a shield.

"Frank?" she asked again.

The floor on the landing creaked and the shadow shifted to reveal a tall man with a full beard in dusty black clothes and a worn cowboy hat.

A sob of terror broke through her throat as the figure closed in on her, forcing her to backpedal until her back was flat against the mattress.

Chapter One

2016
Jess

JESS PACED THE OLD wooden porch. She wasn't entirely sure it was structurally sound. She counted at least ten boards that needed replaced, and it listed a little too far to the left, which only added to her annoyance. It was cold, she didn't want to be here meeting the stupid contractor, with his stupid late face, for this stupid project, on this stupid porch that was probably about to crumble beneath her and drain her of even more of her money.

She checked her watch again. Jess should have waited in her car, but now she was too agitated to sit. Pacing the decrepit porch might just keep her toes from freezing off. It was only the beginning of October. Was it supposed to be this cold?

She didn't even want to be in this stupid town. Topeka, Kansas had never been her choice. Sure, her sister lived here, and so did her cousin, but it was where Ana had moved when her firm had gotten the capitol restoration project, and stupid lovesick Jess had followed her girlfriend. She'd quit her six-figure corporate marketing job and had gone freelance to do it. And she'd been dumb enough to go in on this B&B idea

7

with her cousin, who was the first real client she'd had in this town. But Nell was just so sweet and convincing that Jess hadn't been able to tell her no.

Buying this stupid house had seemed like a good idea in February. The world had been looking up. Jess's business had turned a profit for the first time, the old house had been on the market for a steal, and Ana had volunteered to help with renovation plans.

Jess had felt like she hadn't had anything to lose. Nell could renovate and decorate a showcase house for her interior design business while Jess could document the renovation process and drum up excitement for the finished product. When the construction was done, they'd have a functioning bed & breakfast business that people would be chomping at the bit to stay in.

Except Nell's contractor friend had given Jess the heebie-jeebies. The first time they'd met, he hadn't stopped staring at her. His eyes had bugged, and he'd gone pale and then just kept staring like she was a ghost or a monster. It had been creepy.

Jess had been able to avoid meeting with him since then. She hadn't even been supposed to take this meeting today, except Nell's wedding dress fitting had been moved and absolutely everything came after Nell's wedding plans. Jess loved Nell, not only as a cousin; she'd been one of her best friends her entire life. It was nice having her close, especially since she didn't have any friends left in Kansas City, but she would never get why women got stupid about their weddings. It was just one day. She'd rather concentrate on the life that came after.

Jess had always assumed that she and Ana would spontaneously decide to go to the courthouse one day. They would have just finished a pleasant lunch at the Indian restaurant and would be holding hands in the car, and one of them would suggest swinging by the courthouse to see if there was a judge with an open slot who'd do them a solid since they were downtown already.

That was before, of course.

Jess stopped pacing and looked out over the historical neighborhood. Theirs was the only falling-down house in the vicinity. It shouldn't have taken them six months to convince the neighborhood association to restore this house, just because they wanted to use it for business. It's not like a B&B was going to be noisy. It would probably be rented out to visiting lobbyists or businesspeople. It would be frequented by guests who would literally be there to sleep, grab a scone and a coffee, and leave in the morning.

And it had taken months for the permits to clear.

God, why did everything have to be so hard?

Tears welled, and Jess blinked, willing them to recede. The last thing she needed was the stupid, creepy contractor seeing her break down. He was probably already intimidated by a tiny woman who made more money than he did. No reason to give him any more motivation to be a chauvinist and giving him the crying lesbian would do just that.

No. She stopped, opening her eyes and correcting herself. She wasn't a lesbian. Jess was bisexual, and that had always been the problem. She'd probably still be with Ana if she wasn't attracted to men too.

To distract herself, Jess pulled out her phone and texted Nell that the contractor was late, which was going to make Jess late for an appointment at the new boutique downtown, and Jess wasn't taking any more meetings with the contractor.

Nell's reply—*Ah, give Matt a chance. He's actually really sweet. I promise*—chimed on Jess's phone at the same time a beat-up red truck pulled up on the street directly in front of where Jess stood. When he hopped out of the cab, he was dressed the exact same way he'd been the last time they'd met. Old jeans, threadbare T-shirt, paired with dusty work boots. Dark hair peeked out from beneath a faded red baseball cap, and two or three days of reddish-brown stubble speckled his square chin.

That he was attractive didn't help Jess's mood any. Attractive men had the worst egos, and Jess did not have time to pander to that today.

He stopped when his boot hit the stoop, and he looked up for the first time.

"You're not Nell," he said, cocking his head to one side. He had light eyes, and Jess was pissed at herself for noticing.

"Nope."

"It's Jess, right?" He started up the steps, offering his hand. "Matthew Zimmerman," he said, as if he weren't sure what to do with the way she was glaring at him except to reintroduce himself. After his hand hung in the air empty for a few more seconds, he dropped it, muttering, "What the hell?" to himself, like she couldn't hear him from three feet away.

"You're late," Jess said.

Matthew checked his own watch. "It's only nine-thirty-four. I was two minutes late at most."

"Except you were supposed to be here at nine."

His brows furrowed. "No." He pulled out his phone and scrolled, then turned it around to show her his text thread with Nell. She had indeed agreed to meet Matthew at 9:30.

Jess rolled her eyes. "When she asked me to take this meeting, she told me nine."

"That wedding has completely taken over her brain, hasn't it?"

If Matthew and Jess were friends, Jess might have smiled and agreed, but they were not friends. He was the creepy staring guy, and her toes were cold, and her nose, and how wasn't he freezing just standing there in a T-shirt?

"Yeah, I guess," Jess said. She gathered her giant blanket scarf tighter around her neck and shivered.

"I'll confirm next time." He pulled his hat off his head and ran his fingers through his hair before replacing it. He had gray peeking through over his ears, and Jess wondered how old he was. He didn't look old enough to be going gray.

"Anyway, I wanted to confirm some measurements, make sure nothing has shifted since we were in over the summer. Maybe get a set of keys so we're all set to start on Monday," he said, and Jess realized that he was waiting on her to unlock the door.

It hadn't even occurred to her that she could have waited for him inside. It wouldn't have been any warmer, but it would have been out of the wind at least. The house was so old and in such bad shape, the idea of being inside it alone freaked her out. If she fell through the floorboards, who knew how long it would take someone to find her.

"Sure, yeah." She pulled the keys out of her bag. "I have some photos to take anyway."

Matthew held the screen door, which had no screen and hung on only two of the three hinges, for her while she unlocked the heavy, ancient front door. The lock stuck, and she could see him start to move forward before she got it open. "Like, before pictures?" he asked.

"Kind of. I'll be documenting the whole renovation process for the blog and social media."

"That's right. Nell said you run Twitter or something."

Jesus, was that supposed to be a joke? Jess coughed as they stepped into the front room. A musty, rancid smell washed over her along with the still, cold air. "I own my own promotions company," she wheezed. "It did not smell like this in here last winter."

The last time Jess had been in the house had been on the tedious day the previous February when Nell had dragged Naomi and her here to get Jess's approval. Naomi, Jess's older sister, had just been along for the ride, but Nell hadn't been able to hide that she wanted Naomi's professional opinion about the investment.

Naomi was what Jess liked to call "internet famous." She had huge followings on all the social media platforms, a subscription-only website, and a thriving merchandise line. She had started out giving intuitive tarot readings and called herself a witch. She'd built herself a witchy empire, and basically anytime Naomi came out with a new program, product, or offer, her community threw their money at her. And Nell had kept asking Naomi questions that weren't questions, like, "It's going to be so beautiful and successful, don't you think?" and "Isn't this the best way to start our empire?"

Naomi had said something about how if they could get past the squirrel problem, they'd be golden, and Nell had taken that to heart. That had been when Nell had been promising that the investment on this project would ensure both she and Jess were booked out for years. But it had taken so long to get the project moving that Jess had long ago decided she would have been better off if she had taken the money and hired a couple of assistants instead. Especially now that she didn't have Ana paying half the rent anymore. She needed to be taking on more work, having more revenue coming in, not shelling out thousands to a pain-in-the-ass contractor.

"We had a problem with squirrels in the attic over the summer," Matthew said. "One fell down into a wall somewhere and couldn't get back out. Because I couldn't get the permits pushed through, I couldn't open the walls up and get rid of him." He held his arms up like a magician who'd just performed a trick. "Hence the smell."

Jess waved her hand in front of her nose. She was a skeptic, but score one for her sister and the squirrels. She could have done without the contractor's attitude though. It wasn't her fault the neighbors had put up a stink about getting the house rezoned as commercial. She'd worked as fast as she could.

Ignoring him, Jess pulled her camera from her shoulder bag. The windows, though dirty, were letting in the perfect sort of hazy light to get haunting, melancholy photos of the abandoned building. She felt better now about putting off this photo session. She'd procrastinated on taking the "before" photos, part of her hoping she'd wake up one morning and the whole project would have magically disappeared.

She'd been so absorbed in her work that she didn't hear Matthew approach until he said, "Kind of gloomy 'before' pictures compared to what you normally post, huh?" from just to her right. She was shooting a cobweb-laden built-in bookshelf separating the dining room from the formal sitting room.

"Excuse me?" she asked as she turned to face him. He stood closer than she'd expected, and she took a step back. Maybe next time she'd make sure Nell came with her so she wouldn't have to be alone with this guy.

"I like to know who I'm working for," he said as he pulled out the tab on his measuring tape. "And this is just about the last wall I need to check."

Of course it was. Jess hadn't even finished on this floor. And she was running out of time. She'd have to come back later to shoot the upper floors.

Matthew's arms were stretched overhead as he took the measurement on the doorway when he asked. "So, I assume you'll be in and out taking photographs throughout the whole renovation process?"

"That's how blogs work, yes. Is that a problem?"

Matthew made a note on his wrist with the pen tucked behind his ear and turned to face her, eyebrows raised, hands in pockets. "Not if you respect the rules of the jobsite."

Seriously? She was paying him, and he wanted her to follow his rules?

"Which are?"

"You wear a hard hat and boots when you're on the site, even if we're not actively working."

Jess looked down at her new gray suede, heeled booties.

So did Matthew. "Those don't count."

Jess rolled her eyes. "Fine. What else?"

"Any of my guys who don't want to be photographed don't get photographed. Those that do, sign a release giving you permission to use their image."

Jess nodded. That was easy enough. She had that document on file. "Anything else?"

"Zimmerman-Dartmouth gets credit in each blog post with a link to our website, plus a mention once a week on the social media outlet of your choice."

Jess cocked her head to the side. "That's mighty close to free promotion, Mr. Zimmerman."

A grin pulled up his lips, and he rocked on his toes. "Yup."

"You want me to do all that to get a few pictures while still paying you?"

"That's the deal."

Jess glared at him, but he just smiled blandly back until she gave in. "Fine."

"Pleasure doing business with you, sweetheart." He stepped in too close and pushed back a coil of curl that had fallen over her eye.

Jess hopped back and batted his hand out of the way. "Are we going to have a problem?"

Her heart raced, and she knew her already pale skin was stark white. She hadn't actually been worried about being alone with this man earlier, but now? How mad would Nell be if Jess fired her friend on the spot?

Jess watched Matthew inhale, and take a step back, raising his hands in the air. "No, ma'am."

Good. No smart quips. No excuses. No apologies. Only a contractor who thought he could pull some misogynistic bullshit realizing that he could lose this job just that quickly.

Jess turned on her heel and stopped in the doorway that led to the entry and tossed the keys at him. "Do what you need to do. I'll send you the promotional addendum to our contract later today."

He caught the keys and said nothing, but she could feel his eyes on her as she went to hide in the kitchen to regroup.

Matthew

SHIT. GODDAMN FUCKING bullshit.

He'd touched her. That shiny, curly black hair had been enticing him since he'd arrived. Matthew hadn't had time to prepare himself for Jess's presence. He needed time to remind himself of a few things where she was concerned, but Nell hadn't warned him Jess was taking this meeting instead. In the meetings he'd had with Nell, the way she'd talked about Jess nonstop made Matthew feel like he already knew the woman. That along with some internet stalking had ignited his little candle flame of a crush. And she'd been professional as hell. He'd tried to be. Had possibly used up his bravado for the week with his bargaining, but when he'd driven up and seen her standing on the porch looking pissed, God had he wanted to see if she'd had breakfast yet. Maybe they could discuss the plans more in-depth over coffee?

One of the things he wasn't very good at reminding himself about was that Jess wasn't going to be into him because one, she was in a relationship, and two, that relationship was with a woman. So he needed to stop acting like an entitled asshole.

When she was out of sight and he could hear the shutter on her camera snapping away in the kitchen, Matthew scrubbed his hands over his face, then adjusted his cap. He didn't blame her for being a little hostile. She didn't know him from Adam. And really, he had no business touching her. In his head, he knew it, had been yelling at himself that she wouldn't like it. He'd been watching himself do it as if he were outside his body.

It would not happen again.

This contract was more important than a woman—more important than his embarrassment at his actions or at her blatant rejection.

Matthew recorded the measurements he'd scribbled onto his wrist in his phone, then snapped a few photos. He tried to justify to himself what he'd done and pretend it was no big deal, but all he could hear was his sister telling her four-year-old son that he didn't have to hug anybody he didn't want to. That it was his body and no one else, grandma or no, had any right to touch him if he didn't want to be touched.

Matthew was on the second floor, pretending to check the level of the hallway he already knew was crooked as he tried to formulate an apology that was both effective and sincere without being pathetic.

Heavy footsteps on the stairs going up to the attic forced every other thought from his mind. He looked down the hall, trying to figure out how Jess had gotten past him *and* closed the door without him hearing her, when Jess rounded the corner from the servant stairwell on the other side of the hall.

She'd started to ask him a question when he shushed her. She frowned, but he pointed overhead as the sound of footsteps sounded again on the stairs. They were heavy, reminding him of his dad coming home late at night, cowboy boots creaking on the old wooden stairs.

"You hear that?" he asked her.

But Jess's eyes were on the ceiling, a frown wrinkling her brow. Damn, he was even attracted to her eyebrows. Matthew swallowed as he fought the temptation to trace them with his fingertips.

"Is there someone else here?" she asked in a whisper, sliding across the worn wooden floor to his side without a noise.

He shrugged. "It's an abandoned house, but we've made sure it's locked up pretty tight every time we've been in."

The footsteps stopped, then a lighter set came, like a woman's quick step. Jess's frown deepened.

"Oh, this is ridiculous," she said. She wrapped her big black and white sweater tight around her waist like it could shield her and started for the stairs.

Matthew kept himself from grabbing her arm, but only just. "What are you doing?"

"We can't have people squatting in here when you're about to tear the building apart."

And before he could do anything about it, she was tearing up the stairs with her own quick steps, hollering up about this being private property and offering to find the couple a way less shitty place to live. When she reached the top of the stairs, her call abruptly cut off, and Matthew thought he might be sick.

First he'd touched her uninvited. Now he'd let her run into a potentially dangerous situation on her own. If there really were squatters upstairs, they could have weapons out, ready to defend their space.

Matthew tore up the stairs after her, only to come upon an empty apartment, save for the beautiful, confused woman turning in a circle in the middle of it.

"There's no one here," she said.

"Are you sure?"

"Unless they're hiding under the bed." Jess pointed at the large brass bed frame on the far wall. It had no mattress and was the only furniture left in the room.

"There's a closet and a bathroom." Matthew was already striding toward them, careful not to brush against Jess as he passed her. But both were empty.

"Odd," he said.

"Has that ever happened to you before?" she asked.

Matthew only shook his head. "You?"

"Never."

"Huh."

"Maybe it was the squirrels again?"

Matthew nodded. "It must have been," he said, but in his mind, he was telling himself that unless the squirrel was 200 pounds and wore cowboy boots, there was no way in hell squirrels were making that kind of racket.

"We'll call it squirrels for the day, but you might want to think about a security system."

Jess gave him an incredulous look. "While there aren't any walls?"

"Know any mean dogs?"

"I'm more of a cat person."

Matthew had to hold in a laugh. Of course she was. "Starting Monday, we'll be here full-time. Vagrants shouldn't be a problem."

"Vagrants? Not all homeless people are criminals."

Matthew ground his teeth. "Right. Well, if you're done, I need to get going."

Jess checked her watch. God, it was hot as hell that she still wore a watch.

"Shit. I'm late," she said and set off down the stairs, hollering behind her to message Nell if he needed anything else.

Chapter Two

Jess

ALL THE STRESS OF BEING late for her 10:30 appointment was for nothing. The woman who owned the boutique was on the phone with a sales rep for ten minutes after Jess had busted her ass to get there on time. It was good Jess had the extra few minutes to compose herself, because she was annoyed as hell. Partly because she hated when people kept her waiting, partly because the arrogant son-of-a-bitch contractor still had her creep alarms wailing full blast.

But Jess was a professional, so she took the time to browse the store, examine their displays, and think about who the shop's target audience might be. Usually Jess had no trouble focusing, especially when the client carried cute accessories and trendy clothes. Jess found a whole rack of gray plaid blanket scarves that were just her style, but she couldn't shake off the contractor's cocky grin—or the suspicion that the noises they'd heard hadn't really been squirrels.

There weren't a lot of things that scared Jess, but not really being alone when she thought she was was high on the list. And she didn't even want to think about where whoever it was had disappeared to. There had to be some hiding spot she and

Matthew weren't aware of yet. But shouldn't he have seen the blueprints? Shouldn't he know every hidden corner of that big old house?

Just to be sure, Jess texted her sister. If it wasn't squirrels, Naomi would know, right?

Back last winter when you said we needed to handle to squirrel problem at the B&B, you didn't mean squatters, did you?

Naomi had texted back, *I don't even know what you're talking about. You have squatters?*

You tell me. I thought you were the psychic one.

Intuitive. There's a difference.

Jess shook her head. She loved her sister, but she was definitely a nut. Fortunately, there was a display of leather earrings to distract her. A silver pair in the shape of diamonds caught Jess's eye.

When Jess left the boutique an hour later, she had a new pair of earrings and a much-improved attitude. Once the owner had gotten off the phone, she was lovely and sweet and full of good ideas she didn't have the time to implement herself. Jess had a feeling that they were going to have a very prosperous relationship, and that put Jess in a very good mood indeed, despite the stupid contractor and a text from her sister that said she was going to do a tarot reading for her. That was basically Naomi's version of *I'll pray for you.*

Since she'd skipped her morning planning session at her neighborhood coffee shop, Jess hopped in her silver Prius and decided to head there now, sticking as close to her usual routine as she could.

One thing Jess had learned when she'd gone into business for herself four years before was that if she didn't establish a schedule, she wouldn't get anything done at all. Some people wanted to work from home so they could hang out in their pajamas all day and take leisurely lunches. Jess flat-out laughed in those people's faces. She was up every morning at 5:30 for yoga, followed by breakfast and a shower. She always, always, always dressed for the day, moussed her hair, and did her makeup like she would for any other job—well any other job that didn't ban skinny jeans.

Jess was normally at the coffee shop working from her usual table until ten. Then she had client meetings or returned phone calls through lunch. Then she moved back to her home office and focused on social media campaigns in the afternoons. Before Ana had moved out, Jess would break at five and make dinner and eat with her girlfriend. Now, Jess usually ate standing up in the kitchen, then dedicated an hour or two to answering emails after she'd had a couple glasses of wine to soften her email voice. She'd been told more than once that she came off cold and pissed-off in emails. Apparently writing tipsy made her sound normal.

The coffee shop had just opened for lunch orders when Jess got there. She ordered a grilled cheese with a side salad and a large coffee, but she didn't expect to eat it. One of the myriad consequences of going through a break-up was that Jess had no appetite. In the weeks since Ana had moved out, Jess had already gone down a whole pant size. She had finally achieved that waifish look she'd always desired, but she didn't feel any triumph in it. Mostly, Jess just felt lonely.

The relationship with Ana hadn't been perfect, but she'd had someone around, someone to share things with, and that had been nice. The problem was that Ana hadn't really been around as much as she should have been. When it came down to it, Ana cared a lot more about being a successful architect than she cared about being a good girlfriend. She'd called Jess "needy" for expressing her desire to set aside time together.

Ana had also never been comfortable with Jess's sexuality. She'd told her over and over again that sleeping with guys in college didn't make her bisexual, just curious. And high school boyfriends didn't count either. Hardly anyone their age came out in high school. Jess had stopped arguing after a while. What was the point of arguing the difference between lesbian and bisexual or anything when she was in a long-term relationship with a woman? She'd loved Ana, had planned to be with her forever; who cared what their relationship was called so long as they loved each other?

But there had also been a rebellious piece of Jess, which had become a lot more vocal since the breakup, that was convinced that asking her to deny that piece of her identity was a solid and thorough rejection of who she was at her core. Jess knew she was more than her sexuality, but it was a still a piece of who she was, and denying that part meant not being her whole self.

Jess understood that it was Ana's own insecurity that had let her say those things. On some level Ana was afraid she wasn't enough for Jess. But Jess was already coming to realize that she wasn't responsible for fixing her ex-girlfriend's fears. Ana had been afraid Jess would cheat on her with a man, and nothing Jess could say would ever have convinced Ana that she wouldn't.

Monogamy had never been a problem for Jess, but Ana grew jealous if she had lunch with any man who wasn't her father. Even if that man was a client, Ana would pout about it for days, claiming that she didn't feel like enough to satisfy Jess. She had flat out started telling Jess that she was going to cheat one day, like it was a foregone conclusion. And she hadn't stopped when Jess had asked her not to talk like that.

Then they'd started spending less time together.

Jess worked later into the evenings.

Ana spent weekends at the office, and stayed late most weeknights, until Jess started to suspect that she was seeing someone else.

Jess still wasn't sure if it was true, but when Jess had asked Ana, it had sparked the fight that had ended with Ana packing a bag and going to stay with her sister. Jess had asked her not to come back the next day.

Nell, Jess's mom, and Naomi had all said that Jess was too good for Ana. It was sweet of them, but it didn't make Jess any less sad about the loss of a five-year relationship.

Jess's favorite table at the coffee shop was still open, so she set up her laptop and plugged in her phone. She adjusted her headphones, blocked her email program, and got to work on writing up a proposal for the boutique while the store was still fresh in her mind. Her sandwich was delivered, but at the end of three hour's work, she'd only managed to eat all the tomatoes off the top of her salad and refill her coffee twice.

When she was ready to go, the grilled cheese was still sitting on its plate, looking dry and congealed, but she couldn't bring herself to just throw it away. The morning baristas would have brought her a to-go box by now, but the afternoon baristas were content to ignore her as their after-school crowd rolled in. Jess finally joined the queue to ask for a box. Her mind was still so wrapped up in the proposal that when someone stepped up close behind her and asked, "Can I buy your coffee?" she jumped and let out a little yelp.

She turned with her hand over her heart at the same time Matthew said, "Oh, Jesus. I'm sorry."

Jess took him in. He was dustier than before, and he chewed his bottom lip as he waited for her reaction.

"I'm on my way out," she said. It was finally her turn in line, and she asked for her box, Matthew still hovering behind her.

"How is it I've never seen you here before?" Matthew asked a heartbeat before Jess asked him if he was following her. "I come here every day when I get off work."

"I come in to work in the mornings. I've never been here in the afternoon before."

The barista handed Jess the box and then raised her eyes to Matthew with familiarity. "We're trying out a bean from a new little farm in Costa Rica, wanna try it?"

Jess was surprised when Matthew asked which region and started discussing coffee varietals with the barista. She excused herself to pack up her sandwich, and neither one seemed to notice her absence, but when Jess passed the counter on her way out the door, she heard him tell the barista to hang on and chased her out the door.

"Jess!" he called after her. "Jess, wait."

She stopped and turned to face him, hoisting her laptop bag more securely on her shoulder. Now that he had her attention, he grew shy, avoiding her eyes.

"Did you need something?" she asked.

"Yeah." His voice was breathless, like he had run more than a few steps to catch up with her. He took off his cap and ruffled his shaggy red-brown hair before shoving the hat down over the tousled mop. "I wanted to apologize for earlier. For the thing with your hair. My sister says I'm shameless when there's a beautiful woman in the room, and of course, she's right. It was unprofessional of me, and I want you to know that's not how I usually conduct business."

Jess heard everything he said, but it left her feeling numb more than anything else. She could have been flattered, more likely offended, but she couldn't even drum up indignity at his presumption. She only said, vaguely addressing the air over his left shoulder, "I don't like to be touched."

"It won't happen again."

Jess nodded, and tried to pull off a smile, but she was pretty sure all she managed was a grimace. "I'll see you Monday, Matthew."

He nodded, and she could feel his eyes on her as she left.

Matthew

WOULD HE NEVER NOT make a fool out of himself in front of that woman? He'd already done it twice in one day, so probably not.

He'd chased her outside the damn coffeeshop and babbled an apology while she'd stared at him like he was an idiot. She couldn't have made it any clearer that she wasn't interested in him. Matthew *knew* she wasn't interested in him, so he should probably let it go and try not to make any more a fool of himself than he already had.

Matthew went back inside and collected his coffee, chatted with a couple of the afternoon regulars, and made his way back to his truck. He wrote a few notes in the binder he kept on current projects. The binder lived between the seats in his truck. He kept a lot of his business information in his truck so he had what he needed on him no matter where he was. The Zimmerman-Dartmouth Construction office was at his sister's house. Dana organized the sub-contractors and fielded most of the phone calls, as well as keeping their books and maintaining their website. Matthew joked that she was really the one in charge even though he was the one with the contractor's license. He worked with his crew; she did everything else. And it was time for their daily meeting.

She and his nephew, Jackson, lived in the townhouse they'd moved into after Rob Dartmouth, Dana's husband, had been killed in a motorcycle accident. Rob had been Matthew's best friend and business partner too. He'd been the one with all the business acumen, the one with all the drive. Rob had been the reason Zimmerman-Dartmouth had been so successful. Matthew had just been happy to draw up plans, to oversee his crew, to do the building work, but finding clients and lining up work had never been his strong suit. He preferred to hole himself up in his little two-bedroom house and write most of the time, but in the last two years, he'd learned how to be a businessman. He'd had to. The business was his sister's only livelihood now, and he was proud he'd worked it out so she could work and stay home with her son.

On the drive to his sister's, he tried to concentrate on the plot of his current novel project. He'd been writing a mystery series for the past several years. The first one was scheduled to be published in a couple of months, and the publishing company had asked him if he had any more. They were in negotiations for a series of three, but he was currently working on a fourth book with the same amateur detective protagonist. If the first couple sold well, he was hoping to finish out the series with seven books before he moved on to another project.

Matthew had been writing his entire life. It's what his degree was in. He'd thought he was going to be a journalist in school and had started working construction as a summer job in college because he'd needed money, and Rob had put in a good word for him. The construction job stuck, but the world of journalism was in such turmoil by the time he graduated, he'd opted to take the contractor's exam with Rob and start their own business together instead. He'd always enjoyed writing more when he'd done it for himself anyway.

He couldn't keep his mind on the book as he drove, and he realized once he'd arrived that he'd forgotten Dana's latte. He offered her his pour over. She'd rolled her eyes and pulled a Diet Coke from her fridge before joining him back in the dining room to go over the schedule for the next week.

After Matthew left his sister's house, he'd head back home, shower, and settle into the office he'd created out of the spare bedroom to write until either hunger or exhaustion forced him to stop. Many nights, he forgot to eat dinner. Most nights, he wrote until he couldn't hold his eyes open and he wasn't entirely sure he was making any sense.

It was lonely, putting his writing over having a social life. Matthew was fulfilling a drive, a compulsion, by writing every evening, but it also meant he didn't date a lot anymore. It was too bad, because once upon a time, he'd been good at dating. Every once in a while, after he'd just finished a manuscript, he would go out, meet someone, and enjoy himself, but he'd never met anyone that was more important than his next book idea.

That's how he'd gotten to be thirty-six and still single, even though he'd had every intention of starting a family by now.

For a Zimmerman, he was practically ancient to still be single and childless. Matthew had been born when his parents were only seventeen, and his grandparents hadn't been much older when they'd had Matthew's father. When Matthew graduated college with neither a wife nor a child, it was something of a family joke. He'd always just shrugged and said Rob had taken care of that for him by marrying Dana. But Dana had suffered miscarriage after miscarriage before she'd finally had Jackson. And then to lose Rob so soon after their parents. He wasn't sure how his sister functioned some days. Matthew's stomach still turned sour when he remembered those early days after the accident.

Blaming his lack of a mate on his books sounded better than admitting out loud he had trouble drumming up enthusiasm for anything more than the occasional hookup when everyone he loved died anyway.

Dana and Jackson were the members of his very non-traditional family, and it worked for them. They even still had an aunt who lived on the old family farm near Wamego. That was enough. He'd been telling himself it was good he could pour all his energy into his books instead, and then he'd watched Jess walk away from him twice in one day. Her story had become more important than any of his. What had happened to her to make her the monochromatic woman who didn't like to be touched?

Matthew needed to find out.

He understood he could only be her friend. Or, at least, he was certain he could convince himself of that with practice, but he thought he might like to be her friend.

Now if only he could salvage a friendship after he'd completely freaked her out.

The thought of fear reminded him of the incident with the "squirrels" at the house. He'd been mulling it over in his head all day long. The author in him wanted it to be ghosts. The rational part of his mind knew that there was a better explanation.

He'd worked on houses the owners had claimed were haunted before. Banging pipes were usually just old plumbing. Scratching could usually be attributed to rodents of some sort. Creaking really was the house just settling. But Matthew had never heard something so like footsteps without later finding a person to go with them.

Chapter Three

July 1908
Mary

MARY HAD ACTUALLY BEEN enjoying her afternoon when Frank had arrived in the attic apartment. The look of longing in his eyes when he'd entered the room had excited her. He crossed to her, disrobing as he went. Then he'd joined her on the bed where she waited, covered only in a thin sheet. His heated eyes had met hers from where his head was nestled between her legs.

Mary stretched back on the bed as Frank kissed every inch of her body until she'd tingled all over. Then he'd hovered over her, his mouth on her as his fingers tucked between her legs. He'd taken his time, teasing her until her skin was covered with a layer of sweat and she was panting and begging for him.

When Frank settled between her legs, he whispered words in her ear that normally would have made her blush, but only had her encouraging his hard, frantic thrusts. She closed her legs around his waist to keep him close as she felt her core tighten and pulse, and when the white light of pleasure washed over her for just a minute, she could imagine she was with Wolf again, and the pain stopped.

But then Frank had collapsed on top of her a moment later, peppering her shoulder and neck with kisses. His hot breath still brushed heavily against her cooling skin. He'd said, "I am going to make you my wife, Mary."

It had been the first time he'd ever mentioned it. Mary should have known it would be their eventual outcome. Frank was a serious man, a genuine one. He wouldn't take up a relationship with her without meaning to marry her. It was one of the reasons she'd gone with him the first time he'd asked her to take a drive. She'd have to remarry eventually, but Mary couldn't muster any enthusiasm for it. The excitement that had kept her awake the night before her wedding to Wolf was nowhere to be found. It was enough that Frank was a good lover and would take care of her just as carefully in the rest of their lives together.

What more could she ask for?

Frank wanted to get married in the fall, after the corn was in and he had the extra money to buy them a house. She'd thought the idea would give her comfort. He'd been her lover for months already. They should marry. It was only right.

Only, the thought filled Mary's body with trepidation so thick, her limbs tightened, and she was afraid her tendons were in danger of snapping. Marrying Frank would mean that she was truly, finally giving up on Wolf. He'd been missing for almost a year. And she had to think of her future.

That's what both her uncle and Frank told her every time she had to make a difficult decision. As if leaving the farm and coming to the city hadn't been difficult enough. Their house would be the first place Wolfgang would return to if he ever did come back.

Mary thought she had been giving up hope, little by little. First when she'd had to have him declared dead to be able to put the farm up for sale. Then when she'd taken Frank as her lover. Mary had thought each action had been one step of letting go of her love, but Frank had just left her bed, and he wanted to marry her in the fall, and she knew she hadn't let go of Wolf at all.

The idea broke Mary's heart all over again.

She had fallen in love with Wolfgang the first time she'd met him. She'd barely been sixteen, and he'd come up to their porch one evening, a mongrel of a dog at his heels and his banjo slung over his shoulder. Her father had thought he was a traveling musician at first and had told him they didn't house vagrants. But then Wolf had pulled the deed to the property just to the east out of his pocket and explained in his broken English that he was their neighbor, and he was there to introduce himself and trade a plate of food for a few songs, and Mary's mother had put a stop to any caution and invited him in.

Mary hadn't been able to take her eyes from him, though he'd only been polite to her.

He was tall and looked strong in the thin way people who'd just traveled a long distance always did. His hair was overlong, his beard was too thick and bushy, but his eyes had been kind when he'd smiled shyly at Mary. When her mother had insisted he sit for a haircut the next day, a handsome man who was perhaps ten years older than Mary had emerged from the scruff.

The first thing she'd said to him was that one of her hens was broody, and he was welcome to any chicks that hatched to help him start a flock. He hadn't understood her, and so she'd led him to the hen house and showed him the chicken on her clutch of eggs, then mimed the chicks running by walking two fingers over her palm.

He'd smiled and said, "Yes, *Maus*. Thank you."

"Mouse?"

Wolf's cheeks had turned pink over the top of his newly trimmed beard, and he'd ducked his head.

"The chickens sometimes eat mice, but mostly we let the cats take care of that. You probably need one of those too. The cats are mama's favorites, but I'm sure there's a good mouser or two she'd be willing to part with. If not, I'm sure the Jenson's to the west have—"

Mary had turned to search for a cat to send him with, even though she wasn't even sure he had a house to take the cat back to, but Wolfgang had taken hold of her elbow in his gentle, but firm, grip.

Amusement shone in his eyes, though Mary knew all he could read was confusion in hers. "*Maus*," he said again, then touched the tip of one tentative finger to Mary's nose.

"I'm a mouse?"

He nodded, a tentative smile curling his lips.

"And that's a good thing."

"*Sehr gut,*" he said.

It was Mary's turn to blush, and the curiosity she'd felt the day before bloomed into full-blown infatuation.

The romance had developed slowly and gently, over months of Mary and her mother coming by to help set up his pantry and plant and tend his kitchen garden while her father and a few of the neighbors helped him build his house.

Slowly he'd acquired his small herd of cattle, and he brought her family milk when he had more than he could use.

Mary had a block of her favorite cheese aging in the larder, made from his milk, to give him for Christmas. It wasn't an intimate gift, but she hoped he would understand the connection to the nickname he'd given her. Only when the cold weather came, Mary's mother grew ill and slipped away one night before the doctor was due back in their area.

Her father had taken refuge in the woodshop, building the coffin, then, when that was done, out in the barren fields, finding whatever work he could to do in the frigid cold. It had been Wolf who gave her comfort in those days. He who allowed her to weep on his shoulder, who kissed the top of her head and whispered rolling German words she didn't understand.

She'd been supposed to be baking bread on the day he gave her her first kiss. He'd brought the milk, and she'd rushed into his arms, because she'd barely been able to keep from dripping tears into the dough she'd been kneading. He'd taken her up and let her cry, then sat with her afterward. She hadn't kneaded the bread enough, and it was rising on the counter instead of in the pan. She was just thinking that tough, ill-formed bread seemed fitting enough for her grief when Wolf said in English, "I will miss your mother. She was a good woman."

His accent was thick, and his words had strange edges to them, but that wasn't important. She'd never heard him speak more than a word or two of English at a time, let alone two whole sentences.

Mary pulled out of his embrace to look into his eyes. "You're learning English!"

He grinned enough so she could see the dimple in his left cheek. "A little."

Mary felt the impact of that smile all the way to the very core of her bones. There was nothing in the world that meant more to her than this man's smile.

"Thank you, Wolfgang," she said. "For allowing me to grieve."

His expression turned serious as he cupped her cheeks with both hands. He touched his lips to her forehead, and Mary held her breath, afraid that if she breathed, she would wake up find she'd been dreaming. How many times in the last few months had she dreamed of Wolfgang kissing her?

Wolfgang kissed the tip of her nose.

Then, he'd said, "My mouse," and touched his lips to hers in a short, gentle kiss.

Mary's heart had nearly beat out of her chest, and she'd jumped up to see to the bread, because she knew that even being alone with Wolfgang in the house would be frowned upon.

Wolfgang watched her work for a few minutes, then rose and came to stand next to her. He brushed some flour from her cheek and said in his usual mish-mash of German and English something that she took to mean, "I will speak to your father? Yes, mouse?"

Hope welled in Mary's chest. Finally, something to look forward to.

She nodded, and he kissed her on the forehead once more before leaving.

Only before Wolfgang returned the next day, her father had also taken ill. He went as quickly as her mother had, and Mary was all alone.

After her father had been laid to rest, Wolfgang had taken her hand and asked, "You will come home with me?"

She had agreed. Mary couldn't go back to her parent's house. She and Wolf were married the next day.

She'd only been seventeen, but Wolf was her light in a world full of grief and darkness. He had become her entire life.

They had lived together in his log cabin for almost four years. He'd raised cattle, and they'd still planted her father's fields with grains. The little kitchen garden Mary had planted with her mother tripled in size. It had kept her busy most of the day in the warmer months. Mary was able to sell excess food along with eggs at the market in the nearby town.

But her favorite time had been when Wolfgang would sit next to her in their rockers on the porch as the sunset. Wolf would smoke his pipe and then play his banjo. He didn't sing, but Mary didn't mind. She just enjoyed listening to the music. His fingers were so nimble on the strings, that there were times it almost sounded as if there were two of him.

And when he was done playing and the sun had gone down and Mary couldn't see her sewing anymore, Wolf would lead her to their bed.

Wolfgang had introduced her to pleasure slowly, patiently, tenderly. Mary hadn't been naive, but she hadn't been prepared for the breadth of sensation Wolf was able to wring from her body. She still grew homesick, thinking of his hands on her in the darkness, his lips whispering words in her ear, her hands in his hair, the two of them finding pleasure in each other.

The only thing that would have made their life more perfect would have been a child. But conception had proved to be trickier for Mary than she'd expected. Still, she'd tried to be patient. She was young. She had plenty of time for growing their family.

Mary hadn't been worried when Wolf and the other ranchers left on their yearly cattle drive. It wasn't far to the nearest railhead. They were generally only gone for two weeks, maybe less if the weather was good and there were no stampedes to take them off course. Plus, her uncle lived in Topeka, right near the railroads, so Wolf always had a place to stay.

Only, Wolf never came home that year. The men said they'd assumed he'd decided to stay in town an extra few days. They'd gotten a good price that year, and he wouldn't have been the only one. But Mary heard about the rest making it home without incident. And still Wolf never came.

Her uncle had confirmed that Wolf had been there, had stayed at least the usual two nights, but he hadn't seen him after dinner on the third.

For three months, Mary waited for him to arrive, waited for word from her uncle that some evidence of Wolfgang had been found. Mary had been determined to wait, determined to stay on the farm and raise the child Mary had never had a chance to tell Wolfgang about.

Her uncle was helping her to sell off her father's farm through a lawyer in the city so that she would have something to live off while she waited for Wolfgang to return.

Then she'd started to bleed, and bleed heavily, and she had never been so afraid to be alone.

Mary, growing weaker and more frightened by the minute, saddled her horse and rode without seeing through her tears to the minister's house; his wife, Josephina, was the closest thing they had to a midwife, their little village too small for a proper doctor.

Mary did not remember very much of the next few days. She remembered the lamp on the bedside table and the beef broth she was all but forced to drink. She remembered being too weak to get out of bed for days at a time. She remembered that Josephina had said that her sons were taking care of the horses and the cattle and that Mary should rest and not worry.

But all Mary could do was cry. She had lost everything. First her parents and then Wolfgang and then his child. For a few days, she'd wished the miscarriage had killed her. She'd wanted to die. Living had felt too difficult.

Mary hadn't been sure how she was meant to move forward.

When she was strong enough, she'd left the bed in the spare room and started helping Josephina around the house, then in the garden, and then going out with her to visit other expecting women in the area. The only place Mary did not go was back to her and Wolfgang's farm.

Instead, she'd made plans to stay with her uncle in the city and to work at his lunch counter. It would make it easier to sell the land if she were actually in the city, able to speak to the lawyer and not use her uncle as a go-between. This time, she'd planned to sell it all and make a new life for herself in the city, where she could forget the pain and the loss and the loneliness that she'd suffered in the countryside.

Uncle Levi owned a house two blocks from his store. It was a grand three-story house that he'd built when he and his wife, now deceased, had still planned to have children. They never had become parents, and Uncle Levi had turned the third story into an apartment that he rented out to young gentlemen new to town. The bottom two floors of the house were reserved for himself and his housekeeper, Edie.

When she'd first arrived, Mary heard Uncle Levi tell Edie one morning that "the poor child moves about as if she's a ghost."

Edie said, "She's had a time of it, Mr. Levi. Give the girl some room."

So that's what her uncle had given her. For weeks she woke, went to work at the store, came home, and helped Edie with dinner. She would eat with her uncle, then sit with him in the parlor. He would read while she would work on her knitting or her sewing or her mending.

Of the first three months Mary lived in the city, she did not remember very much. It was cold, but then, winter was always cold. It seemed to snow less than she was used to, but that only made it easier to walk to the store. Once a week, she'd met with Mr. Black, the young new lawyer in town, to discuss the sale of her properties. He'd been kind to Mary. He'd reminded her that with the sale of two farms and all of their assets, she was about to become a very rich lady and could do whatever she liked. That should make her very happy indeed. Mary would only shrug and look out the window onto the cold streets and the frozen wagon ruts, like scars in the mud.

It was not until the apple trees outside her bedroom window at her uncle's house had begun to bloom that Mary noticed her surroundings. It started with the apple blossoms, the scent wafting in through the open window. She had cracked it overnight because, for the first time since Mary had arrived in the city, it had been stuffy in her rooms. When she awoke, the sweet smell had been drifting in on the breeze, and then she'd looked down on the backyard.

When had everything become so green? So verdant?
Mary thought of the city as drab. Brown. Dirty.

But right here, looking out this window, she could almost imagine she was back at home, sitting on the porch with Wolfgang in the evening. He would smoke his pipe, and she would knit him thick wool socks for the winter with wool from the sheep of their friends the Shepherds, who lived on the other side of the village. Mary didn't spin, but Mrs. Shepherd was happy to trade yarn for fresh cream and access to Mary's blackberry bramble come summer.

Mary could almost smell Wolf's pipe as she watched the wind sway the branches of the tree, but the fresh blossoms, determined to become apples, stayed stubbornly put. He would talk to her in German, a language it had taken her nearly a year to begin to understand, and sometimes, she still had to ask for clarification about a word he'd used. Between the two of them, they could usually determine meaning. Mary thought it was a sign of their love that they did not need to always speak the same language to understand one another.

One night, on a spring evening when the grasses in front of the house were just beginning to turn green and the cows were munching every blade they could find, lowing softly in appreciation, Wolf had grasped her hand between their rocking chairs and, with a fond grin, had called her his mouse.

She asked him, "How do you say, 'I love you' in German?"

Theoretically, she knew the words, but she still got mixed up on verb tenses.

"*Ich leibe dich*," he said.

She repeated it twice, trying to mimic his accent.

"Why do you want to know?" he asked.

"Because I love you" was all she said.

Wolfgang squeezed her knuckles. "I know, my little mouse. You do not need to say it."

"And if I want to say it?"

He gestured with his pipe. "By all means."

"*Ich liebe dich*," she said again, and Wolfgang leaned over and kissed her with smoky lips.

Watching the apple blossoms sway outside her window, Mary had whispered, "*Ich liebe dich*," into the wind, and hoped that wherever it was that Wolfgang had ended up, he would hear her. She would always love him, she'd decided, but she could no longer live like a ghost. Wolf wouldn't want that. He would want her to make a life for herself. He would want her to be happy. So she would try to be.

Later that same day, during her meeting with Mr. Frank Black, it had dawned on Mary suddenly just how very handsome he was. And Mr. Black's quick eyes had caught her observing him and returned the admiration with a mischievous twinkle.

Now Frank wished for them to marry in only a matter of a few weeks, and all Mary could think of were those evenings with Wolfgang on the porch. The feel of his hands finding her intimate places in the darkness, and the idea of marrying Frank, made her weep.

Chapter Four

2016
Jess

YOGA HADN'T BEEN SO difficult for Jess since the day she had decided to ask Ana to move out. Even then, when going through her day's affirmation, Jess had known it was what she needed to do for her own peace of mind. Monday morning, Jess woke knowing that she would see her ex-girlfriend for the first time since the breakup.

She'd also had a text from her sister. *You want me to go with you this morning? Rachel didn't work last night, so I don't have to take Oscar to school.*

Rachel was Naomi's roommate. The roommate Naomi had been in love with since freshman year of college, but who was, alas, straight. That hadn't stopped Naomi from moving here to help take care of Rachel and her son after Rachel's husband had died.

I'll be fine.

Yeah, but it's the first time you'll have seen her since she moved out, and I worry about you.

I'm a big girl. I can handle it.

Jess didn't want to tell her sister that she was nervous as hell. She didn't know if that was unusual behavior or not, to have zero contact with an ex after a breakup. It was what came naturally to Jess. Calling or meeting or even fucking hooking up would only prolong the agony. The decision to live apart had been made, and Jess only wanted to learn how to live with it.

Except when Nell had conceived of this project a year ago, they had brought Ana in as the architect, because it only made sense to keep the work in the family, as it were. Ana had been happy to do it, had even given them a discount on her plans. Twelve months ago, Jess had been ecstatic to work on a project with her girlfriend. This morning, it seemed like the worst idea she'd ever had.

She fumbled her way through yoga, barely even remembering to breathe, but reminding herself that she'd showed up to do it, and that was what was important. She washed her hair and hoped for the best as she did her makeup in the style she knew Ana preferred. Not to attract her, just to make sure she noticed that Jess was looking her best, being her best, despite everything. Then she dressed in her new favorite outfit: an oversized white shirt with a chunky gray cardigan and black leggings. She chose her favorite gray suede booties, despite the contractor's disapproval, and a black-and-white buffalo-plaid blanket. scarf paired with her new leather earrings.

She only spent one hour at the coffee shop before loading her camera with a fresh memory card and packing her spare battery, then drove over to the site of the future inn. Matthew and his crew were already there. Nell pulled in right in front of Jess, and thankfully, Ana's car wasn't anywhere to be seen.

Good. Jess had another few minutes to compose herself.

"I thought we talked about the boots," Matthew called as she approached the group milling around on the lawn in front of the porch. They all stared at her shoes.

Having already chosen to play it cool, Jess said, "You haven't started work yet. Besides, they make my legs look hot."

Someone in the group whistled. Another shouted his affirmation. Jess gave them a sweet smile while flipping them off with both hands.

Matthew said, "Careful, fellas. She's one of the boss ladies."

The wolf-whistler sketched a bow. The others laughed when Jess bowed in return and said, "And I won't hesitate to kick any one of you out on your ass."

Nell stepped up beside Jess on the sidewalk and elbowed her in the side, which was almost like elbowing her in the shoulder, Nell was so much taller. Nell was tall and skinny and full of sharp angles. Jess was petite, and while fit, she was curvy and sturdy. The only thing that was sharp about Jess was her tongue.

"Be nice, Jess."

Jess wrapped her arm around Nell. "I'm always nice."

The men had gone back to their previous conversations while sipping their coffees and looking up at the house. Though Matthew was examining something over their shoulders.

Nell linked her long, thin arm around Jess's shoulders. "I love you, but you are mean and scary like the big bad wolf."

Jess pretended to be horrified. "Me? I'm harmless."

"Don't be ridiculous," came a sweet feminine voice from behind them. Jess and Nell turned as one. "We all know you're as harmless as a pissed off mountain cat."

"Play nice, Anastasia," Nell said. "We're here for the inn."

Nell insisted on calling the B&B an "inn," like it made it fancier somehow. In Jess's mind, an inn served more meals than just breakfast. But her mind wasn't functioning fully as she set eyes on Ana. She'd dyed her short, spiky blonde hair redder, like she did every fall. She wore a black suit, her pencil skirt to her knees, and black hose accentuating her long, thin legs down to her tasteful heels. The only thing not conservative about her appearance was the chunky teal and gold necklace Jess had bought her for her birthday only a few weeks before they'd broken up.

Jess tried to think of something to say as Ana stared her down but could come up with nothing. Thankfully, Nell had stepped back and pulled Matthew, who Jess had forgotten was there, into the conversation.

"Matthew, you know Anastasia Moriarty, right?"

Matthew strode forward and offered Ana his right hand. "Of course. Good morning, Ana. You're looking positively gorgeous, as always."

Ana placed a hand possessively on Matthew's shoulder. "Oh, Matt, you big flirt, you'll never get me to switch sides. Now, Jess is a different story. You might be just her type."

Just like that, Jess had plenty to say. "Don't be a bitch, Ana."

All the eyes on the small construction crew came to rest on Jess at the same time. Matthew took one step backwards out of Ana's reach, looking back and forth between Jess and Ana, understanding in his eyes.

"There's that pissed off mountain cat," Ana's voice was a purr.

Nell appeared back in Jess's field of vision. "Stop it, both of you. If you can't behave like adults, I'm firing you both."

Jess knew she couldn't be fired. She owned half the house; Nell would have to buy her out, and Nell didn't have the money to do so. Ana, on the other hand, snapped to attention and shut her lips into a thin line, something she only did when she was mad as hell. Ana didn't get fired. Period.

"Good," Nell said. "Now, we were going to start the day off with photos, so everyone on the steps."

Nell arranged everyone while Jess set up her tripod. When they had planned this day, these photos, Jess had pictured it happy and laughing, with everyone excited to set out on a new adventure. Instead everyone looked stiff and nervous, afraid to step out of line lest Jess or Ana came to verbal blows again.

Jess did her best to cajole and tease. "Come on, you guys look like you're at a funeral. You gonna let a couple of little girls scare you?"

The guy in the red shirt who'd wolf-whistled said, "You are scary, woman."

She did her best imitation cougar howl, and they all laughed. "Perfect. You're all gorgeous. Flex those biceps for me."

To Jess's delight, the whole lot of them struck bodybuilder poses, and Jess captured as many of those as she could. Those would make fantastic promo shots.

"Okay, you guys are officially the best construction crew I've ever worked with," she said.

A few of the men preened a little bit.

"Don't get too cocky now; you're also the only construction crew I've ever worked with. Now make room for me in the front." She set the timer and ran to the steps so she was in at least one of the photos. Then she got one with just Ana and Matt, then some with just her and Nell, then a couple with all four of them.

Originally, Jess had planned a shot with just her and Ana, a happy photo of them with their arms around each other, smiling and excited.

She skipped those, choosing instead to head inside and catch a few shots of Ana and Matthew going over the plans on a sheet of plywood over two sawhorses. Ana wore a hard hat, even though Matthew left his on the table, holding down a corner of the blueprints. It was staged, because of course they had already planned everything, but the photos would look great, and even better, Ana left as soon as they were finished.

Jess shot a few of the guys setting up their equipment as the prepared to demo the first floor, then got a photo of Nell doing the ceremonial first hit with a sledgehammer into a water-stained plaster wall. She made a small hole in the plaster, a cloud of dust spraying up from the mallet and sprinkling onto the floor.

Matthew took the sledgehammer and held it out to Jess with a smile on his face, pure and genuine. "It's your turn, mountain cat."

Jess laughed as Nell handed over her hard hat and safety goggles. "You don't happen to have a silver hat, do you?"

Matthew shook his head, and Nell plopped the yellow hat over Jess's black curls. "It won't kill you to wear some color, now come on."

Jess traded Matthew her camera for the sledgehammer and took a swing at the wall while he photographed her. Without trying to, Jess left a hole in the lath too.

She laughed as she lowered the head of the sledgehammer to the floor. "Damn, that felt good."

"Great swing," Matthew said, trading her back her camera. His smile was amused as she shunted the hard hat underneath her arm and flipped through the photos he'd taken of her.

"These are great! Nell, look at this one, the sunlight catching in the dust looks almost ethereal."

Nell hunched over Jess's shoulder. "Oh, wow, Matthew, are you a photographer in your other life?"

Jess looked up just in time to see Matthew lift his ballcap, run his hands through his hair, and resituate the hat.

"I just hit the shutter," he said, and noticing Jess's eyes on him, his sheepish smile turned to something else. His eyes were blue, Jess noticed, and they looked at her like she was a goddess come to life.

Jess felt a shock race through her. When had anyone last looked at her like that? Thankfully she was saved from thinking about it any further when Nell shoved the camera back under her nose.

"Hey look at this. Doesn't that look like a face in the dust?"

Jess took one last glance at the tender look her contractor was unabashedly sending her way and then focused on the screen in front of her.

"Whoa, crazy." In the cloud of dust that had billowed over Jess's shoulder was a pattern that looked vaguely like a man's face. "I wonder if he was the one we heard walking around the other day." Jess held out the camera to Matthew. "What do you think?"

He said, "I think it's a trick of the light," at the same time Nell asked what Jess meant by hearing someone walking around.

She looped the camera strap over her head and fluffed her hair. "When we were here last week, we thought we heard something in the attic. It was probably squirrels. No big deal."

Nell looked from Jess to Matthew, who shrugged, and back to Jess again. "You don't think someone was in the house, do you?"

"Definitely not," Matthew said. "I checked the place over inside and out, just to be sure."

He hadn't told Jess he'd come back and done that, but why should he? She'd given him the keys so he could do just that—and really, Nell was the lead on the project. If he'd really suspected anything, he would have contacted her. And if this was the first Nell was hearing about the incident, then it probably meant Matthew really hadn't found anything to worry about. The squirrel excuse still sounded flimsy to Jess, but she couldn't think of what else it could possibly be.

Chapter Five

Matthew

MATTHEW HAD DISTRACTED himself over the weekend with meaningless mundanities. Cleaning, running errands, playing his banjo. Bringing Jackson and Dana donuts. He did have a deadline, but his editor had given him more time with these last sets of revisions than he strictly needed. And he'd been too restless to sit at his desk. Laundry, grocery shopping, double-checking his supplies and the work schedule for the new project, raking leaves in his backyard, none of that was enough to distract him from the woman who had been on his mind since Friday morning.

For longer than that if he was honest with himself. It had been easier to ignore his attraction to Jess when he'd only seen her the once and hadn't had the chance to interact with her. It had been easier to pretend before he'd seen her teasing his crew, seen the utter devastation she hadn't quite been able to hide when Anastasia had shown up.

Matthew hadn't known they'd broken up. Though, he supposed Nell would have no reason to share her business partner's relationship status with him. He and Nell had never had more than a cup of coffee while discussing what type of molding to put in the living room. The only personal information he knew about her was that she was getting married next year, because Nell always found a way to work her wedding into the conversation, and that Jess was Nell's cousin, and that Nell basically worshipped her. Nell talked more about Jess than she did about her wedding. He knew Jess's parents were eccentric, and Nell had stayed with Jess in the summers, and they'd spent the whole time getting burned to a crisp at the pool. He knew Jess had a sister, but he hadn't known Jess was single again.

Not that it mattered to him.

A foolish, hopeful part of him had thrilled when Ana had mentioned that he was Jess's type, even though he hadn't missed the maliciousness behind it. Clearly Jess having a type that wasn't Anastasia wasn't supposed to be a good thing.

And yet.

Matthew sat down at his desk and opened his laptop. He stared at the blank screen, not able to help the small smile that crept over his lips as he said his secret out loud, admitting it to himself for the first time.

"Jess looks just like Clarissa."

She looked exactly like the character in his book. It was as if Clarissa had walked off the page, into a trendy boutique, and then right into his life.

He'd noticed the resemblance before, of course. He'd probably spent months of his life contemplating that character's motives, appearance, the subtleties of her personality. The way a quirk of an eyebrow would change the contours of her face. How the hardening of her gaze could shift her expression from open to accusing in the space of a moment.

Matthew had told himself that he'd been imagining the similarities the first time they'd met. A petite brunette with curly hair and intense gray eyes was a basic description of a lot of women. But the other morning, Matthew knew the reason he couldn't keep away from her was because she looked so much like Clarissa that his stupid mind couldn't stop thinking of her as *his* Clarissa.

His protagonist spent about half the first novel switching between trying to work out if Clarissa was the murderer and lusting after the sharp-tongued PR agent in her smart suits. In that regard, Jess and Clarissa were nothing alike. Jess's casual, trendiness was the one thing that kept reminding him she was her own person and not the character he'd been writing for the past six years.

Clarissa had dangled her affection like bait for Tate Fischer through three books now, remaining tempting, yet elusive, just out of Fischer's reach. Matthew had a feeling that if he wasn't careful, Jess could become his real life equivalent. As much sense as the unrequited love made for his mystery series, Matthew was not keen to reenact any parts of his novels in real life.

Matthew would do well to remember real life. Because in reality, Jess was not Clarissa. She was her own woman with a unique past who had just gotten out of a long-term relationship with a woman.

Matthew would keep reminding himself of that important fact until it stuck. As much as he wanted her to be, Jess was not straight. She was still mourning the loss of her girlfriend. The last thing she needed was a commitment-phobic hermit, whose longest relationship was with his laptop, making her feel uncomfortable.

He'd leave her alone and concentrate on his work, and the crush would slowly fade into the background. It would have been better had she not figured out how he felt this morning. Matthew knew she'd seen on his face something of the admiration and affection he'd felt while watching her smash up the wall. She hadn't hidden her shock well—and if that hadn't been admonition enough, she kept well out of his way for the rest of the morning and didn't meet his eyes again at all before she left.

It was only a little humiliating.

Matthew had even avoided going to the coffee shop that afternoon, just in case she'd decided to work there again after being on site all morning. And really, that coffee shop was his territory. Anthony, his best friend from college, owned it. They didn't talk as much as Matthew would like, but that was because Anthony was always travelling to remote parts of the world, searching out new and better beans and negotiating direct trade deals with the farmers. Coffee was pretty much all Anthony talked about when he was in town, but that was okay with Matthew. He was interested—had even had Anthony walk him through the roasting and cupping processes. It had earned him the coveted spot of being invited over for tastings whenever Anthony came home with a promising new batch of beans—and it threw baristas for a loop when the guy covered in sheet rock dust knew more about coffee than they did.

Matthew went to bed Monday night resolving to keep his distance from Jess until he could be around her without making a fool of himself. Then, first thing Tuesday morning—well, first thing for Dana, which was after nine—when he'd already been on the job site for a couple of hours, she called and asked him if he could bring her coffee beans on his next break. She knew that while he spent much of his time on the job site, he also was the one to run all the errands and take all the meetings, so he was running around town as often as he was actually doing the work.

He cursed to himself, because the minute Dana had called, he'd known Jess would be at the shop. So much for keeping his distance. Now he just had to keep his resolve to let her be. This would be his first test.

Sure enough, the second Matthew came in the front door, his eyes scanned the dining room only to find Jess staring right at him, as if she'd known he was coming. She wore headphones, and a different variation of her monochromatic wardrobe, having switched out her usual oversized sweater for a black blazer and her blanket scarf for a white gauzy one.

Matthew nodded in her direction, suddenly self-conscious about the hole he'd torn is his dusty blue T-shirt that morning. She smiled in return, inclining her head ever so slightly, before returning her attention to her computer.

That was how their interactions proceeded for the next several weeks, polite, friendly, brief. Matthew never once stopped feeling as though he'd been struck by lightning the second they started occupying the same space, but making distinctions between the real Jess and the fictional character who looked like her became easier.

The trouble was, Matthew didn't like her any less. She teased the crew without hindrance or remorse. She and Nell seemed to share a genuine closeness, even when Jess rolled her eyes at being asked to choose between two almost identical shades of blue paint. Jess even skillfully dodged any mention of Anastasia, who she had avoided meeting on the jobsite again, even though Jess was around far more often than he'd expected her to be in the beginning.

Matthew had met with Ana a few times and had been too much of a coward to ask what had happened with Jess. Then again, Ana didn't invite casual conversation easily. She was severe enough to be strictly business all the time.

Then he reminded himself that Jess's past was absolutely none of his business and would go look for his favorite hammer again. He should be worried about his own memory issues, or who in the crew was messing with his toolbox, because he was tracking the hammer all over the damn inn.

Jess

IN THE FEW WEEKS SINCE the renovations on the bed and breakfast had started, Jess had made great progress toward feeling more like a human being and less like Ana's personal emotional rag doll.

Jess had started the autumn waking up each morning with failure pressing into her chest like a ten-ton weight was attached to her ribs. She'd known that breaking up with Ana had been for the best, but that didn't make Jess feel any better about ending a five year-long relationship. It had made her miss what their relationship had been at the beginning. Because there had been a time when Ana had made Jess feel special, loved, supported. Jess probably wouldn't have had the courage to start her own business if not for Ana's constant cheerleading.

Maybe their relationship would have been different had Ana been as supportive of every part of Jess. It was not a coincidence that Ana had encouraged Jess to start her own marketing company when it enabled Jess to move with Ana. When it came to supporting things that didn't benefit Ana? That was another story.

How often had Ana discouraged Jess from traveling for a conference, telling her how to invest her money instead. She'd thought the B&B was a terrible idea until Jess had asked her to be the architect on the project. Jess knew that would be the only way to live with her if Jess was serious about the investment. Otherwise the sideways comments about wasting her savings would have slowly eroded Jess's confidence in the project and undermined the whole thing. It had been Ana's continuous comments on Jess's sexuality and the eventuality of her cheating someday that had sabotaged Jess's confidence in their relationship to begin with.

The renovation project had turned out to be a blessing in disguise. As awful as it had been to actually get to the renovation, Jess enjoyed being at the jobsite and seeing the house come together. She liked chatting with the guys on the crew, and the pictures of the process had become the most visited post every week on her blog. And, maybe it had a little bit to do with how at home Jess felt with herself while she was in the building.

She didn't understand it entirely, but when she was there taking pictures, goofing off with the guys and stealing their donuts, Jess felt more like herself than she had for years. Like, since none of them knew her, they had zero expectations of who she was supposed to be, and it was easier to be herself with them than it was even when she was alone.

At least when she was with other people, she didn't have to think about the parts of her that she was still unsure about. Except it wasn't that Jess felt unsure about her sexuality. She knew she was bisexual. That she'd found herself staring at Matthew's ass in the last few weeks only reinforced that. But was she comfortable living that outwardly?

Jess didn't know.

She didn't think she was ready to be with anybody. She'd even gone out looking for a hookup and met up with a girl she'd gone out with a few times before she'd met Ana. When she'd asked Jess to come home with her after a couple drinks, Jess hadn't been able to see it through.

It was like Jess had somehow lost all her sexual confidence. Ana's compiled list of snide remarks about Jess leaving her for a man, about how she wasn't a real lesbian, since she was attracted to guys, or how she wasn't really bisexual because she hadn't been with a man in a decade, they'd all built up in Jess until she didn't have any confidence in that part of herself at all anymore.

And then there was Nell, always pushing Jess out of her comfortable existence. She'd cajoled Jess and Naomi out tonight. She'd said she'd needed some girl time with her cousins, but after half an hour of Nell pointing guys out to Jess while Naomi cackled, Nell was now trying to set her up with her fiancé's best man.

"He's super built," Nell said, as she sipped her soda with lime. Sure, they were at a bar, but ever since Nell had met Austin, she'd given up alcohol. The two of them only did things that were healthy. Jess was still rolling her eyes from the first time Nell had explained why there was no longer vodka in her soda.

"When have I ever expressed interest in a man over the way he looks?" Jess asked. She was drinking her usual, whiskey neat. Naomi was more preoccupied with watching the group of guys across the room. Two of them were gorgeous in completely different ways. One was tall with a smile so bright, he could be in toothpaste commercials. The other one was Latinx and appeared completely unaware of the way Naomi, and a good portion of the rest of the bar, were staring at the breadth of his well-built shoulders. "That's the guy Rachel's seeing," Naomi said, pointing at the one with the shiny smile.

"He's pretty," Jess said. Which was true, even if his overly confident body language made him look like an asshole. "What do you think of him?"

Naomi shrugged. "I think he doesn't want to be temporary." Then Naomi shifted her gaze back to the bar where Rachel was working. Jess didn't miss the longing in her sister's eyes, even as she caught Rachel watching the guys too. Jess squeezed Naomi's shoulder.

Nell was on a mission because she missed the exchange entirely. "See, Jess. You don't have to be in a relationship forever. You could have a temporary guy."

"When have you ever known me to be attracted to temporary?" Jess asked.

"This isn't about what you find attractive, it's about using a well-muscled, well-endowed man for his body."

Naomi spluttered out a laugh and high-fived their cousin.

Jess lowered her eyes to her drink. "Maybe I don't want to go out with a guy."

Nell pursed her lips in a false pout. "But I'm no help to you when it comes to women, and I'm tired of feeling so helpless when you're obviously so miserable."

"You are a sad sack these days, Jess," Naomi threw in as Jess leaned forward over the table and sniffed at Nell's drink.

Nell snatched her drink away. "What are you doing?"

"Just checking you didn't sneak some vodka while Austin wasn't looking."

Nell covered her heart like Jess had wounded her, and Naomi cackled.

"I don't understand what's so bad about wanting to cheer you up." Nell sounded so sincere that Jess couldn't help but laugh.

"What makes you so sure that riding a buff dude will make me feel better about . . ." Jess cut herself off and gestured toward her body.

"I'm not," Nell said, and squeezed the last of the juice out of her lime wedge. "But it's something you haven't tried yet. And it's not like it would hurt anything."

"It's not going to fix me either."

"You're not the problem," Naomi said. "You just need to get your confidence back."

"See! That's exactly what I'm talking about!" Nell raised her glass, and Naomi clinked her gin and tonic against Nell's.

"You two are no help."

"And you're determined to be miserable," Naomi said. "You're stuck."

"Have you been doing tarot readings on me again?"

Naomi shrugged and looked back at the bar, but the tilt of her eyebrows said, *what are you going to do about it?* "I'm just saying, if there's *anyone* that you're interested in. You should go for it. I know the dude who has my vote."

"Who?" Nell and Jess asked at the same time.

Naomi gave another one of her vague shrugs that Jess hated. It wasn't enough for Naomi to be an annoying older sister, she had to always play up the, "I-know-something-you-don't-know angle too.

Jess pursed her lips. Despite her sister's supposed intuitiveness, there were no guarantees. The last time Jess had been with a guy, he hadn't known how to touch her, and she'd been sore for days.

So maybe she was a little hesitant to hook up with another guy. Not opposed to it, but not with somebody she'd never met before.

"Am I really that pathetic?" Jess had thought she'd been behaving more like her old self.

"You're not as mopey as you were at first," Nell grasped for Jess's hand. "But you were withering away under Ana's jealousy."

Jess nodded and sighed. "I was."

"That bitch was killing your spirit."

Jess shot Naomi a sharp look.

"What? I didn't like her from the beginning."

Jess and Naomi had had this conversation before, and Jess did not have any patience for her sister's superiority on the subject. "Just don't, okay."

"And—" Nell cut in before the sisters could stoke an argument, "I was thinking that maybe if you got with a guy, it would maybe help you get over your whole preoccupation with it."

"I think it's actually a really, really bad idea."

Nell drummed her nails on the bar. "You don't think it will help you conquer your demons?"

Jess drained the last of her whiskey. The idea of sleeping with someone just to sleep with them made Jess's heart race while tension knotted her shoulders. "Not even a little bit, I'd just hear Ana in the back of my mind the whole time telling me what a whore I am."

Nell made a snarling noise. "I really hate that woman, you know that?"

Naomi and Nell toasted again, and Jess tried to at least be glad that the two were bonding over her pain but couldn't muster the enthusiasm.

Jess grabbed Naomi's glass and finished that too, then made a face while her friends laughed at her.

They were quiet for a minute, Nell chasing ice cubes with her straw while Jess and Naomi watched Rachel pull a beer for a guy who'd been standing at the bar for ages. He was tall, a little on the skinny side, but with shaggy brown hair that reminded her a little of Matthew's—or at least what Matthew's would look like if he ever went a day without wearing his ballcap.

"I think," Jess said, "that if I ever sleep with anyone, man or woman, again, it will be because there's something there, you know? I don't have it in me for one-night stands anymore."

"I understand," Nell said. She snagged Jess's hand and squeezed.

"Of course you understand. You're getting married. I only deluded myself into thinking Ana and I could get married if I stuck it out long enough."

Naomi let out an inelegant snorting sound.

Nell pointed at Jess with her straw. "That. That sort of talk is exactly what I mean when I say I want to cheer you up. You have got to stop beating yourself up about her. You tried, and she didn't, and when you couldn't take it anymore, you did the best thing for yourself and got out of it. You were the wronged party, and you still somehow let her make you feel like you're the one who did something wrong."

Jess tried to smile but couldn't quite manage it, then buried her face in her hands. "I know. I know."

"But you were trying to say that casual relationships hold no interest for you anymore."

"I'm thirty-two, it's about time I'm done with them, don't you think?"

Naomi shot Jess a look that said that she was older and was definitely not over hook-ups and offended by the insinuation. Jess raised her eyebrows and darted a glance toward Rachel, who was now scowling at the guy with the distracting shoulders. Naomi shrugged in response. She had no defense against how in love she was with Rachel, and no desire to fall out of love either.

That was the difference.

"I think you were done with them a long time ago." Nell said.

"Yeah," Jess said, watching the bartender again. "Maybe you're right."

Maybe it was time to stop beating herself up for being wrong about who her forever person was. Jess and Ana were over. It was time to stop letting Ana's words dictate how she lived the rest of her life.

Chapter Six

Matthew

HAVING JACKSON ON THE jobsite always made Matthew nervous. He loved his nephew, but the kid didn't know how to not touch. He was on top of, inside, or underneath anything he could climb on, hide in, or crawl beneath. Matthew didn't doubt that his nephew would accidentally cut his own fingers off or shoot a staple into his eye out of curiosity.

But Dana insisted on bringing treats whenever one of the guys had a birthday, which meant Jackson was on the jobsite at least once a month, and Matthew could barely pause long enough to enjoy his cupcake for fear of all the ways his nephew might be maimed. He'd done a quick clean-up before they'd arrived, making the guys lock up sharp tools or drills, and unplug the saws.

Still, Matthew was careful never to let Jackson out of his sight.

Today the task wasn't as much of a chore as it usually was because Jess was there, and Jackson was already wearing her scarf of the day, a fluffy thing made of out thick black yarn with pom poms hanging from the ends instead of tassels. Jackson was sweeping around the still mostly empty dining room with the scarf draped over his shoulders, flapping his arms like a bird while Jess took pictures of him being ridiculous.

It had been a long time since Matthew had let himself admire her, but under the guise of keeping an eye on his nephew, he allowed himself the indulgence of noticing the brightness to her eyes, the pleasure of delight with Jackson lighting up her face. Her laugh. The smudge of chocolate frosting that still sat on the corner of her mouth. Matthew longed for an excuse to lick it off. It didn't take much for him to imagine what she would taste like, something fresh, sacred, and light, like sugar and lemon and sunlight tinged with the chocolate from the frosting might possibly be the most intoxicating flavor he would ever taste.

Only Dana had to go and ruin Matthew's fantasy by offering Jess a napkin and pointing out the smudge. Matthew pulled out his phone to pretend he hadn't been staring as Jess blushed and dabbed at her lip. Then his sister turned toward Matthew with her eyebrows raised and a look of accusation in her eye.

"You haven't quite got all the drool yet," she said. "You missed some just here."

She poked one of the buttons on his shirt, and Matthew looked down, only for Dana to flick him on the nose.

Dana cackled as Matthew shook his head to clear the sting from his nose. "Did you actually think you might have been drooling?"

Heat pooled across Matthew's cheeks, and he reached for his bottle of water from where it rested on a sawhorse. "Of course not."

"Uh-huh." Dana bumped him on the hip with her own and said, "So have you asked her out yet?" she asked. Nodding to where Jess was wrapping the scarf around Jackson's neck so it draped behind him like a cape.

"It's not like that," Matthew said. He tried to stand casually, angling his head away from Jess so she wouldn't overhear the conversation.

The way Dana cocked her head to the side said she thought he was lying.

"Okay, so for me it is, but she's not interested."

"How do you know if you haven't asked?"

Matthew hadn't worn his ballcap today, and he wished he had so he could pull it lower over his eyes and hide from the scrutiny that was Dana. She always got like this when there might be a woman in his life.

"Because I know her ex-girlfriend," he said, his voice basically a whisper.

Dana's brows creased together. She looked so much like their mother when she did that. Same dark hair, same all-knowing green eyes, it made Matthew grin despite himself.

"Well, that's inconvenient," Dana said.

"You're telling me." He gave in and shoved his hands through his hair. It was getting too long. It was going to hit the back of his collar if he didn't get it trimmed soon.

"She kind of looks like Clarissa, don't you think?" Dana asked as she watched Jess and Jackson head for the stairs in search of the window seat in the upstairs bedroom.

"Yup."

That made Dana laugh and squeeze his shoulder, like she couldn't decide if she was more amused by or sympathetic to Matthew's dilemma. "Damn, you're screwed, huh?"

"Gee, sis. I can't express my gratitude enough for your understanding."

She tried to rein in her giggles but couldn't breathe. "It's just so like you to fall in love with the one woman who will never love you back."

Matthew shrugged out of his sister's hold. "I'm going to go make sure they're not in any of the rooms with equipment in them."

"Good luck," Dana called after him, still failing to stifle her giggles.

That was all he needed today, his sister's opinion about his crush on Jess. He'd been doing a pretty good job at ignoring it lately. He'd even turned on his dating apps and tried chatting with a couple women. But apparently if you add Jess plus a kid plus chocolate frosting, you got one lovesick Matthew, because he had zero interest in answering any of the messages waiting for him on his phone.

He heard a loud *thunk* as he climbed the stairs and doubled his pace. It was probably just Jackson jumping off the window seat, but he wanted to be sure. His hammer was still appearing in random places, and he was certain he'd seen someone lingering in the bank of windows in the attic more than once, but he'd yet to catch anyone in the house who wasn't supposed to be there.

When Matthew got to the master bedroom, they weren't there.

The sound of laughter drifted down the stairs, and quick little-boy footsteps tripped across the floor overhead. Of course they were in the attic apartment, with its freshly mudded walls waiting to be imprinted with little-boy fingerprints. Matthew hadn't checked the attic earlier. He hadn't even thought they'd go up there; the stairs were so dark and so steep, he didn't think Jackson would even try. Not that Matthew could blame his nephew, he would probably follow Jess to Mordor if that's where she wanted to go. He knew for certain there was a Sawzall and a sander still in there, probably still plugged in. Not to mention spare drywall sheets and who-knew-what-all else.

But when Matthew crested into the attic, it was just Jess and Jackson, twirling together in the middle of the bedroom portion, safely away from the equipment piled on the far wall in the kitchen. They laughed together and both collapsed to the floor—an echo of the thud he'd heard earlier.

Jess's head clearly spun as she pushed herself to sitting. Jackson sprang to his feet and staggered, looking like a drunken preschooler. Matthew caught him before he careened into the empty brass bed frame.

"Hey, Matthew," Jess said. She swayed slightly as pushed to her feet but corrected herself before he could reach her to help. She never had gotten a proper pair of boots. The ones she wore today were giant wedges. It was a wonder she hadn't broken her neck—or an ankle.

"We were spinning, Uncle Matt!" Jackson said as he tugged on the tails of Matthew's flannel shirt.

"I saw that." He ruffled the kid's sandy hair. "Your eyes are still spinning. Going in two separate directions just like a cartoon."

"Eyes don't spin."

"Well, yours are," Matthew said, but Jackson was already appealing to Jess to find out if his uncle was lying.

Jess was doing her best to dust off her black jeans and said, "I don't know, Jack. I think *I'm* still spinning."

Then all three of them looked to the stairwell as heavy footsteps climbed the steps. Only no one emerged, and the hairs rose on the back of Matthew's neck as he remembered that first day he and Jess had been here together. He hadn't heard the footsteps since.

Jess peeked into the hallway, which was still dark, but the bulb in the light fixture had been replaced at least. She pulled on the chain. The light came on, and Matthew knew there was nothing there.

The footsteps started again, the sound of boots climbing the stairs on repeat. And then the swift, light set of footsteps skipped across the room, just like they had the first time, and Matthew could have sworn he felt the air around him stir with a chill as the footsteps passed where he and Jackson stood.

"What was that?" Jackson asked.

Jess shivered as the footsteps dissipated right at the point where she stood. She met Matthew's gaze with frightened eyes.

"Just an old house," Matthew said, patting Jackson on the shoulder. "Come on, let's go find your mom." He herded Jackson toward the door, but Jess didn't move as they approached. She stared at Matthew, her big eyes wide with shock.

Matthew paused next to her. "You okay?" he asked.

"That wasn't a squirrel, Matthew."

He couldn't help himself, Matthew brushed one of her errant, now dusty curls out of her face. "Shhh. We'll talk about it later, okay."

He nodded toward Jackson. Jess took in a deep breath and sighed it out before he realized his hand was still cupping her cheek. She seemed to notice at the same time and looked startled for a whole new reason. Her guarded eyes met his and their gazes locked. Matthew couldn't look away from her. Her big gray eyes seemed to be asking him if he was serious, and in response, his thumb brushed ever so slightly over the curve of her cheek.

Matthew wasn't sure who was more surprised by their silent conversation, him or Jess. He didn't know if she had any inkling how he felt about her. Hell, he'd been pretending that he didn't so much over the last few weeks that he'd convinced himself he was on the verge of being over it. The only thing that kept him from stepping into her space and pressing his luck was Jackson starting down the stairs. If his nephew hadn't been there, Matthew would have put himself just far enough into Jess's space that she would have to be aware of his body, but far enough away that they weren't actually touching. Then he would have cupped her other cheek with his free hand and asked if he could kiss her.

Instead, he swallowed so hard, he almost choked and stepped back far enough for Jess to precede him down the stairs.

She glanced back at him over her shoulder when she hit the second-floor landing, and he could only imagine what his face looked like. Every nerve ending in his whole body fired at once, reaching for some sort of feedback from her, but all he received was the chill lingering in the cold attic air.

Matthew paused on the second floor, listening for any other noise from the attic, but all he could hear was the guys getting back to work below.

By the time he made it to the front porch, Jess's Prius was pulling away from the curb, and he was fighting the sinking feeling in the pit of his stomach that told him he had just royally screwed up.

Chapter Seven

Jess

THE REARVIEW MIRROR was not Jess's friend today. It showed her the dark circles that her makeup didn't quite hide. And her complexion appeared even paler than normal. She touched up her red lipstick, which she'd hoped would make her look more alive, but which she was pretty sure just made her look more corpselike.

She'd tossed and turned all night, and the combination of virtually no sleep and her short-circuiting inner workings had combined to make her the hot mess she was this morning. She probably shouldn't even be at the inn, and definitely not this early, but she couldn't think of anything else to do.

When Jess hadn't been able to sleep, she'd gotten up and done yoga early. She'd showered, answered some emails, put the finishing touches on a client's December marketing plan, and it hadn't even been seven o'clock. So she'd gone for a coffee, and now she was here.

Nobody else was at the house yet. It was too early for the crew to show up. Matthew's truck wasn't there. Not that Jess was waiting for him. She wasn't. Not really.

Only.

She did need to talk to him, and she'd hoped that maybe she'd be able to catch him alone. After what happened the day before, they needed to talk. And it was probably better if they did it sooner rather than later.

The last thing Jess wanted to do was to get out of the car and wait in the frigid cold November morning, but she was too antsy to sit around in her car anymore. She wrapped her scarf tighter, tugged the belt snug on her wool coat, and cupped her gloved hands around her cup of coffee.

Jess shivered as she huddled behind one of the columns on the porch. It was far too cold for the beginning of November. Her hair was still wet for Christ's sake. If she had to wait too much longer, she'd have frozen hair for half the day.

Thankfully, Matthew's old red truck pulled up behind Jess's Prius a few minutes later. Like always, his eyes found hers without having to search. A smile spread over his lips, and he jogged up to the porch, a brown Carhartt coat unzipped over his usual T-shirt. He hadn't even added the red flannel shirt she'd noticed him wearing on the coldest days. Wasn't he freezing? Jess was wishing she'd dug her wool beanie out of the closet this morning too, but it hadn't been worth the effort when it would only squash her hair. Cultivating her curls was a delicate routine that a hat could kill even on the best of hair days.

"What are you doing out here?" he asked, heading straight to unlock the front door. "You'll freeze to death." He opened the door and gestured for Jess to proceed him in. "Or at the very least catch a cold. Come inside."

"Yes, Mom." Jess said with a sarcastic roll of her eyes as she went inside. It was no warmer than it had been out on the porch, but the floor was littered with space heaters. Matthew hurried around the two front rooms, switching them on, rubbing his hands together in between.

"So, what are you doing here?" he asked, joining her in front of the most powerful heater, where the first waves of warmth pulsed weakly through the cold air. The way his friendly grin faltered for just a second let her know he was hiding behind the same feigned geniality he'd been operating under the past few weeks. Jess had to give it to him, he was good at pretending. He'd almost fooled her.

"Waiting for you, I think," she said as casually as she could, her eyes on the glowing coils beneath their hands.

"Me? Why?" His strangled voice told Jess that he knew exactly what she wanted to talk to him about, and that he wasn't nearly as good at the acting casual game as she was.

Jess shifted from one foot to the other, pretending she was shifting her feet to stomp warmth to her toes instead of procrastinating because of incoming awkwardness. When she looked up, he was staring at the red creeping over the coils inside the heater.

"Because, if I'm not mistaken, I think you have a crush on me."

Matthew's eyes snapped up to meet hers, the flash of panic on his face giving him away without his having to say anything.

Jess couldn't help it, her lips spread into a grin as a little thrill bubbled inside her at the truth that this man wanted her. "A big, fat one, too."

The rigid position of Matthew's shoulders' dropped, as if someone had sawed the tension off him when he realized she wasn't going to give him a hard time. "Guess it's pretty obvious after yesterday, huh?"

Jess shrugged. "I mean, I suspected before, but yeah, yesterday was pretty much a dead giveaway—unless you do that cheek cupping thing with everyone."

"Nope. Boss or no, I'd probably get my hand cut off that way. That or teased mercilessly."

She didn't mean to, but Jess giggled thinking about how the guys teased one another in her presence, far less vulgarly, she was sure, than they were when she wasn't around.

"I'm still not sure why you're here," Matthew said when they'd lapsed back into silence.

Rubbing her hands together in the now potent waves of heat emanating from the space heater, Jess said, "Did you know that Anastasia and I used to date?"

He frowned at her. "I put it together, yeah."

"Dating makes it sound less serious than it was. We lived together for more than four years. About three months ago, I kicked her out."

"Yeah, Nell alluded to you two having been serious. I'm really sorry."

"Yeah, well, a person can only take so much sometimes, you know?"

Matthew nodded. "Soooo, what did you want from me?" He, too, was looking at his hands as he warmed them over the space heater. They were cleaner than Jess expected them to be. His long, strong-looking fingers, as of yet unmarred by dust or dirt, though his knuckles looked raw and dry. She wanted to reach into her bag and hand over her entire tube of hand cream.

"Nell's been trying to set me up with random guys, a sort of rebound situation, I guess, but I just kept thinking about you."

Matthew issued a half-strangled croak as he jerked back a step.

Jess laughed. "Not like that. Don't worry, I'm not looking to take advantage of your crush."

She could feel his eyes on her, running up and down her frame, not checking her out so much as checking to make sure she was the same person he'd been working with the last few weeks.

"I can't say that I'd mind all that much, I just didn't think . . ." he trailed off.

"That I fucked guys?"

He cocked his head to the side. "Sure, you could put it that way."

Jess ignored him, not wanting to get into the finer points of her sexuality at the moment. "Mostly I was wondering if you knew about my relationship with Ana and had a crush on me anyway, or if you didn't know—and if it changed how you felt about me after I told you."

Matthew shoved his hands in his coat pockets and focused on a point over her eyeline as he said, "I've tried to forget about it. Apparently, the fact that you prefer women has absolutely no bearing on me, so I've resigned myself to suffering in silence until we're done with this job."

"God, you're sweet," Jess said.

A flush stole over his cheeks, and Jess grinned. He was sweet, and a little shy—at least when it came to talking about his feelings. "I'm glad that's the way you see it. Do I want to know why you're asking?"

"I've dated men before—well, more like boys, it's been so long—but it was something Ana never let me forget."

Outwardly, Matthew's expression didn't change, but she felt the intensity of his eyes as he focused in on her again, taking her in for the first time as a bisexual woman. She almost saw the switch flip in his mind from *off-limits* to *possibility*. "I see" was all he said.

Jess's heart beat too fast. Did he see? That she was confiding in him. Not because she was looking for a rebound or a hookup, but because he'd made her feel seen yesterday, and she just wanted to tell her secrets to someone who might listen to her and hear her truth without judgement.

"I haven't admitted that I can also be attracted to guys in a long time." She bit her lip and made herself look up at Matthew, who looked like he didn't dare breathe lest he scare her off. That was something. "I kind of felt like I had to erase that part of myself to keep Ana happy, because she felt threatened by it. Even though I would never—" Jess cut herself off when Matthew nodded. "Anyway, Nell keeps trying to set me up with dudes she knows so I can get comfortable with that part of my sexuality again. She thinks that I won't get over Ana until I do, but I have to keep telling her that I'm not ready to sleep with anybody."

If Matthew had any opinions about what she was saying, he didn't let them show on his face. Jess did see him inhale, which was good. She had absolutely no clue what to do if someone passed out. He also didn't say anything, which made things super awkward.

"Sorry, I needed to talk, and for whatever reason I thought you wouldn't mind listening."

Matthew closed his eyes and pulled his lower lip between his teeth as he rubbed a hand over the stubble on his chin. "Thanks, I guess?" he said.

Jess winced. She'd just made everything worse by trying to be honest with him. She didn't blame him for being confused.

"Right." She let out a long sigh. "Well, I had been hoping maybe we could be friends. Or try hanging out outside of work sometime. But I can see how that's probably not going to work for you, so I better get to work."

Jess turned on her heel, wishing she hadn't worn shoes that made such a loud clacking noise when she walked. Normally she loved that noise, it made her feel powerful, but now it just highlighted that she was walking away from someone—again.

She was almost to the front door when he called, "What kind of friends?"

Jess turned around and took a few tentative steps back toward him. "You know how sometimes you come into the coffee shop while I'm there, and you always get your coffee to go?"

"Yeah."

"Maybe you could sit down with me sometime? Tell me where you learned so much about coffee. Or you know, we could discuss the ghosts in the attic."

Matthew's chuckle was deep and half-reluctant, but the ghost comment had won the smile she'd been after, even if it didn't reach his eyes. "I could do that."

Jess could make out the dent of a frown between his eyebrows, but he wasn't saying no, so maybe that was something.

Chapter Eight

Matthew

SWEET.

Jess thought he was sweet.

Matthew had never particularly thought of himself as sweet. Puppies were sweet. Kittens. Cookies.

He was not sweet. Understanding? Yes. Capable? Yes. Intelligent? Absolutely. Masculine? Definitely. Maybe he could even pull off rugged with his work-hardened hands and construction-honed muscles. So maybe he was a little taller than he was broad. Maybe he had a secret double life as a mystery author, but that shouldn't soften him enough to make him sweet. If anything, it should make him intriguing.

Matthew moved a few of the heavier pieces of equipment into the master bedroom, where they would begin their reconstruction of the second floor, just because he could. Though massive, rebuilding the second floor was going to be tricky. There was only one bathroom, and even that was an addition. He was going to have to replace old, probably poorly added pipes, and run new pipe throughout so that each of the five bedrooms could have its own private bath.

As he lugged his toolbox up the stairs, Matthew could hear his sister chastising him in his head. *And what do you think you're doing saying you can be friends with this girl?* She would ask. *We talked about this; you need to stay away from her as much as possible, go out more, meet other women.*

He had tried that. He had even met someone on one of his apps, gone out on a date with her, but they never got past awkward kisses on the landing outside her apartment. She'd been nice, and she'd tried, but Matthew's heart just wasn't in it.

It seemed if he couldn't have Jess, he didn't want any woman at all.

Matthew stood back and surveyed the tools he'd just lugged up the back staircase. Maybe he was strong, but that didn't mean he wasn't also pathetic, lapping up whatever scraps Jess would send his way. She'd even given him an out, and he still held out hope.

Part of him, the pathetic part, thought that maybe she meant more than she'd said. That maybe she'd asked him to be her friend because she was interested but wasn't sure she should be.

Matthew didn't trust that part of himself at all. That was the part that had latched on to how she'd said she'd dated a man, like a dog with a toy he didn't want to give up.

That small morsel of hope is what made him stop by the coffee shop at every opportunity over the last week, hoping she would be there. He'd gone every day since she'd made her offer, but he hadn't run into her. Matthew wasn't going to give up on what might be his one opportunity to convince Jess he was anything but sweet.

God, he was fucking pathetic.

He'd just come back from an expensive afternoon coffee run for the guys—an excuse to *maybe* run into Jess, who he'd missed again—when Ted said, "Boss lady's upstairs. Showed up right after you left."

Matthew didn't have an appointment with Nell, but she was in and out a lot as she put together the decorating plan. And Jess might need more pictures. His heart ticked up at the possibility of Jess waiting for him upstairs, but asking which one of their employers was upstairs was more of his hand than Matthew wanted to show right now.

"Do we know what she needs?" he asked instead.

Ted shrugged and took a sip of his super sweet frozen coffee, even though it was fifteen degrees outside. "She didn't say, but she brought a lot of stuff in with her. Mac said she set up shop in the attic."

That didn't make any sense. The attic was still a dusty catchall with barely finished walls.

"I guess I better go make sure there isn't a problem."

Matthew half expected to find Nell flitting around the attic with giant bolts of fabric, draping it against the still drying mud as she decided on what color curtains to hang in the big bank of windows. There was a distinct lack of footsteps for that though.

Instead of Nell, Jess sat in the middle of the attic, one of his drop cloths spread out on the floor with a gray and white blanket on top of it. In the center of the blanket, Jess sat cross-legged with her laptop resting on her knees and notebooks surrounding her, like she was in the middle of some office-supply conjuring spell. Her eyes flicked to his as he crested the stairs, but she kept typing.

"Oh good," she said as he entered the room. "There's an actual person attached to those footsteps."

Matthew snorted. He couldn't help it. Every word from her mouth affected him way more than was healthy. "Corporeal and guilty," he said and motioned toward the blanket. "May I?" This wasn't quite the coffee shop, but it might be the closest Matthew ever got.

Jess pushed a couple notebooks aside to make space for him. "You have any more of that coffee?" she asked, her eyes on his to-go cup.

Matthew held it out. He'd already had too much coffee today anyway. "There's no cream," he said, remembering that's how he'd seen her drink it. "But it tastes like blueberries and honey."

Jess's expression told him she thought he was full of shit, but she took a sip of his drink anyway, her lips covering where his had just been. The idea of their lips sharing space was enough for Matthew's blood to thrum in his veins. Then he watched her eyes grow wide as the flavor of the coffee washed over her tongue.

"How do they do that?" she asked, slipping the cap off the cup and peeking inside to ensure it was just coffee that she was drinking.

"It's in how they roast the beans. Anthony's been perfecting this one for the last few weeks."

"Anthony?" Jess replaced the lid and took another sip. "Okay, this is really good."

A slow, leisurely delight settled into Matthew's chest and spread as Jess handed the coffee back to him.

Were they sharing?

Matthew took a sip that he didn't taste because he was too busy noticing the vanilla lip balm Jess had left on the mouthpiece.

Jess was looking at him expectantly as he set the coffee on the blanket between them, and he remembered she'd asked about Anthony. "He owns the coffee shop. We've been friends for about fifteen years."

"And what about the blonde barista?" Jess asked. She had a pen twined between her fingers, even though she'd been typing. It stayed there as she reached for the coffee again.

"Which one?" he asked. Matthew knew the baristas since he went in so often, but they all just gave him good service because they were afraid Anthony would hear about it if they didn't.

Jess was smiling when she said, "The tall one who works in the afternoon. She likes you."

"What?"

"She never takes her eyes off you."

"Rochelle?" Matthew accepted the offered cup and took another sip, pretending he wasn't buzzing at the strange intimacy of sharing his coffee as his fingertips brushed against hers.

"You hadn't noticed?"

Matthew drank, his eyes on Jess's. She obviously didn't think their actions meant anything as she waited for his response.

"I can be a little oblivious to that sort of thing," he said.

But Jess was already nodding, biting her lip again. "I'm not surprised. It sort of seems like you live in your own world."

Matthew felt his face crumple from the flirtatious half smile he'd been wearing into a frown.

"Oh, look at you," her fingertips landed on his wrist for just a second, then just as quickly, they were gone. The electricity of her touch lingered, as she continued speaking. "It's not a bad thing. I only meant you always seem to have something on your mind."

He shrugged. He wasn't sure he was ready to tell her about the writing, and really, half the time he wasn't thinking about his novels. He had his construction schedules to worry about and an extensive to-do list each day. Then there were phone calls and bills and invoices, and even if Dana mainly kept track of those, he still liked to be in the loop. And then of course there was making sure Dana and Jackson were doing okay. No, he definitely had plenty on his plate, so he told Jess about his business partner's untimely demise and how it affected his family and his time.

"I'm so sorry," she said when he finished.

Matthew still didn't know what to say when people said that, but he knew there wasn't much else for them to say. "We're doing all right a couple years in. Dana's my office manager now, which means she can stay home with Jackson like she likes, and I'm still free to act like more of a foreman than a contractor half the time, so I'm happy."

"You don't like being a contractor?"

He shrugged. "I've always liked the physical part of the work—the labor. I've struggled with the business side."

"I could help you with that if you like," Jess said.

Matthew had the nearly empty coffee cup back in his hands again. He did not want to be one of her clients, even more than he wanted her not to be one of his. "How about we don't talk about business."

"Sure," she said, expression still relaxed, almost sunny, even. "Let's talk about our ghosty friends instead."

Matthew checked over his shoulder, like her mentioning the possibility would summon the footsteps. "Is that what you're doing up here? Ghost hunting?"

Jess held her thumb and forefinger up so there was barely any space between them. "Maybe a little bit. Mostly I couldn't stop thinking about these windows." She gestured toward the windows behind her where the golden afternoon sunlight was streaming in. The sun was dipping low in the sky, but Jess looked ethereal bathed in the glow. "But I also wanted to see if the footsteps came back. So far, nada."

"And here I was thinking maybe you were here to see me." Matthew wished he hadn't said it, but he wasn't able to deny the truth to the words.

"Well, the coffee didn't hurt." Did she just bat her eyes? Was she flirting back?

When he tried, Matthew didn't usually have a hard time with women. He wasn't bad looking and owning your own construction business wasn't a bad opener, but Matthew had never been so confused by a woman as he was by Jess.

Every time he met her eyes, she had a smile for him. And through her brilliant smile, she asked, "So have you guys had any more weird stuff happen?"

Since that first time with the squirrels in the attic, some of the guys had complained about their tools going missing and turning up again in strange places, or the battery pack on the drill losing its charge, or the lights flickering sometimes. All of it had happened before on other projects, and every time it was just one of the guys messing around or an old battery or bad wiring. Matthew didn't think it was anything different this time, even the shenanigans with his hammer. And he didn't want to tell her that he hadn't entirely ruled out squatters, because he hadn't seen any proof of any trespassers, only a possible figure in the windows. He did not, however, have any answers for what had happened in the attic a couple weeks ago, or the footsteps they'd heard the first time they were in the house together.

"Drew's hard hat went missing for the afternoon again, but I'm not so sure Mike isn't messing around with him. He's been known to haze the rookies."

"Damn, I was hoping to create a narrative out of it."

"You want people to think your inn is haunted?"

Jess shrugged. "Are we finally going to talk about how it's not squirrels running around up here?"

Matthew raised his eyebrows. "I heard footsteps. I thought a man in boots was climbing up the stairs, like Rob was still around, coming upstairs to talk to me about something. We only brought up squirrels because we didn't know what else to call it."

"Do you think that's what this is?" she chewed her lip like she was afraid to ask, or afraid of how he'd take the question.

Matthew shook his head. It wasn't even a possibility. "Not even a little bit. I don't think anything is haunting your house, but that doesn't mean I can explain the footsteps."

"And what about the second set? It *felt* like something, someone ran right up to me."

Matthew only shook his head. He had tried to forget about that part and focus on the way Jess's skin had felt against his palm.

Jess stared off into the distance. "Maybe I could still do something with it on the blog—just to catch people's attention. Lay out the experiences with no interpretation. Just saying that a couple of strange things have happened will help theories build on their own, which means people will be talking about us."

"And that's really what you want?"

"It's all in good fun," Jess said. Her smile was so bright, Matthew was tempted to imagine a haunting for her.

Chapter Nine

1908
Mary

THE FIRST TIME MARY met Frank, she had accompanied her uncle to a meeting at his office to discuss the sale of her and Wolfgang's land. He had been sitting at his desk, wearily staring at a leather file when he called for her uncle to open the door, but upon seeing Mary, he'd stumbled to his feet, practically tripping over himself as he rounded the desk to greet them.

He wore a dark gray suit, with a jacket slung over the back of his office chair. A gold chain reached from the button of his waistcoat to the pocket, where a fine gold fob watch likely rested. He wore wire-rimmed glasses and was clean shaven. His hair was a light shade of dusty brown so indistinguishable, it almost appeared gray. But he had soft brown eyes and was just old enough for them to be lined around the edges when he smiled.

Mary's uncle had told her that Frank Black had moved to their city only the year before, after finishing his law degree and taking over his ageing father's practice. Frank's father had been a friend of Mary's uncle, and Frank had lived in the attic apartment of their house when he had first come to town. Now he occupied the rooms adjoining the law practice.

"It's nice to meet you," Mary said, nodding back to Frank as he raised her knuckles to his lips and kissed her hand. She'd only read about men doing that in novels. No one had ever treated her so genteelly. Didn't he know she was nothing more than a rancher's widow?

"It's my pleasure, ma'am. I have heard that you've had a hard go of things of late. Please, sit, and tell me how I can help."

Mary and Uncle Levi sat in the two wooden chairs facing the heavy wood desk and explained in depth about the properties while her uncle showed Frank Black what paperwork they had.

"My brother wanted his land to go to his daughter and her family upon his death," he said as he handed over the will and a hand-drawn map of the two properties. "Mary and her late husband were in the process of combining the two farms, as they share a border, but we think we have a better chance of selling them as two separate lots."

"I am very sorry to hear about your husband, Mrs. Zimmerman. You can't have been married for long, I think."

"Four years," Mary said, looking out the window at the drab winter browns. She had not yet woken from her grief, and allowed her uncle to speak with the lawyer on her behalf. She barely noticed when Frank Black kissed her hand again on her way out or how attentive he was at each successive meeting. Mary did not hear her uncle when he complained of never having so many meetings to sell a piece of land in all his lifen—or did she hear his ribbing when he suggested that Mr. Black only wanted to see her as often as he could.

All of the compliments Frank had paid her over the winter landed on Mary's ears all at once that spring day when she whispered her last *Ich liebe dich* into the wind. She ran into him in the street as she headed home from working at the shop. Her apron was stained, and her blonde hair had started pulling out of its coiled braids. Frank was walking the other way down the street, a paper sack under his arm, which must have been the makings of his dinner.

He'd kissed her hand as always and said, "I'm glad to happen upon you. I had a letter today about your parents' land. There is a gentleman who would like to buy it. Would it be acceptable to bring the offer to you tomorrow? I hate to force you out on your day off."

Mary blushed when she realized he had not let go of her hand as he spoke, but stood before her, holding it in the street for all to see. Her uncle's teasing rang in her ears as realization swept down upon her. Mr. Black seemed very much in love with her right now, and maybe he had been since the moment they'd met.

Mary stared at their clasped hands, nearly forgetting his question. Did she want Frank Black to be in love with her?

"Mary?" he asked, and she met his gaze and noticed his tender smile.

"Yes, Mr. Black. That would be perfectly acceptable."

"It's just Frank," he said. "Please."

Mary smiled at him and pulled her hand from his. "I will see you tomorrow, Frank."

When she thought back on it, that had been the start of their affair. Mary hadn't meant to begin one. She had thought they would go about things the proper way, but when Frank's offers to take her for a drive moved from innocent conversation to sneaking off to steal kisses to ever escalating physical passion, Mary had not complained. It seemed exactly the distraction she needed to forget her grief.

Mary looked forward to their encounters, though they were different than things had been with Wolfgang. Wolfgang had always been tender with her. He moved his large body slowly on top of hers until she was wet with sweat and panting with need. Then he would kiss her from shoulder to shoulder and unleash himself, like a crescendo at the end of a symphony, leaving them both breathless.

Frank was a different sort of lover. He was methodical in touching her so that she gave in to ecstasy at least once before he entered her. It was pleasurable, no doubt, but as much good as Mary derived from her encounters, she knew that the difference between intimacies with Wolfgang and Frank were that she had loved Wolf and valued his touch. The most she was prepared to say about Frank Black was that she was fond of him, even if he did know how to wring pleasure from her every pore. Frank was more of an addiction than anything else, and while she expected him to marry her one day, Mary did nothing to hasten the subject along.

Only as summer began to wane, Frank mentioned it more and more often, and not just when they were alone. He invited her to sit in his pew every Sunday at church, which was how the town found out about their courtship, which meant they had to spend more time in public together. They spent less time in the attic and more time driving together or dining together in the evenings. When Frank came to the sandwich counter, he would ask her within hearing distance of the others when she was going to make an honest man out of him.

Mary's cheeks burned every time, and she never had a chance to tell him she'd never objected to his plans to marry in the fall, just had never agreed that they should marry in September.

Before long, the whole town was acting as if the date had already been set. The preacher even came in for lunch one day and asked when a good time would be to set up an appointment to go over the wedding ceremony She'd only told him that she wasn't planning a wedding.

That didn't stop anyone else from planning the wedding for her. Every day Edie had a new treat for Mary to try, wanting to know if she should make it for the wedding reception.

The final straw had been when Mary was on her way to Frank's office after work and the dressmaker ran out her shop's front door and stopped Mary in the street to confirm their appointment for the day after next.

"It's a tight turnaround," she said. "Only four weeks, and Mr. Black will want you looking perfect."

"Yes," Mary said. "I'm sure he will." She was about done with the entire town making decisions for her.

Frank was still sitting at his desk when Mary let herself into his office.

"You made me an appointment at the dressmaker's?"

Frank looked up without raising his head, making eye contact over the rim of his glasses. "Well, you'll need a wedding dress."

"I have a wedding dress." She still had the dress she'd worn when she'd married Wolf. She still wore it on special occasions.

And Wolf had always delighted in bring her fabric and patterns she had no use for on the farm, simply because the process of sewing them delighted her. She'd made three other dresses over the years that were just as nice as the first.

Frank pushed his glasses up his nose and rose from his seat, a scowl pinching his mouth. "I won't marry you in a dress you wore while marrying another man."

"I haven't said I would marry you at all."

His boots sounded heavy on the floorboards as Frank crossed the room to stand in front of her; his hands gripped both her arms, not enough to hurt, but more firmly than he'd ever held her before. "Mary, I know you miss your late husband, but if we don't wed soon, you'll be carrying my child before I have a chance to save you from that ridicule."

Frank's hold gentled, and he brought one hand to her cheek as if he were going to kiss her, but Mary said "I don't conceive easily" before he could.

A narrowing of his eyes was her only clue that Frank hadn't thought of it before. "How do you figure?" he asked.

"I was married to Wolf for four years and am childless." She did not add that it wasn't because they didn't try, because they had. Fervently. Mary was not keen to test the bounds of Frank's temper, especially not in his office. The buildings were so close, the street just on the other side of the door. Mary had a feeling that when something set Frank off, the neighbors would hear it. She had little doubt that calling to mind the image of her enjoying marital relations with Wolfgang would be like opening the gate on a bull.

"Well, perhaps I am more virile than your last lover," Frank said. This time he did kiss her, as if he needed to make a show of his potential potency then and there.

Mary stepped free of his embrace. "I'm not ready to remarry, Frank. It hasn't even been a year. Can we please at least wait until a year has passed?"

"You'll need my protection before then," he said.

"I told you, it's unlikely that I will be with child any time soon." It had taken her four years to conceive with Wolfgang, after all.

Frank moved closer, boxing her in against the door. "I don't just mean in case of children." He leaned in, his nose grazing her ear as he inhaled the scent of her. Mary always thought she left work smelling of meat and dill pickles, but that didn't seem to deter Frank at all. He pressed his body against hers, his eager manhood pressing into her belly.

"You'll have the money from the sale of your land soon, and I care about you too much to watch someone take advantage of you." Frank kissed down the curve of her neck as his other hand reached around her waist and turned the lock on the door.

Mary had never felt less affectionate than she did right now. She didn't want Frank's kisses. She wanted to know about her land.

"You sold it?" she said, pressing against his chest.

Frank worked on the buttons at the back of her dress to loosen the neckline. "The sale for your parent's land is almost finalized. And I have a buyer for the ranch."

Mary's heart clenched. She didn't want to sell the ranch. She'd always wished she could keep it as a memorial to her husband. "You have a buyer."

"Yes, my love. And once the land is gone, you can put your past behind you, and we can move forward together."

Together.

The word echoed through Mary's whole body as if she'd gone hollow, and there was infinite space for the syllables to reverberate within her.

Together with Frank. A man so completely different from Wolfgang, a man with soft hands and a clean-shaven face and who she didn't love.

Was this really the best way forward with her life?

Mary didn't have any answers, and because she didn't have any answers, she let herself fall into the feel of Frank's hands on her body. But that's all it was, physical release, barely even strong enough to banish her sorrow at the idea of selling Wolf's farm.

When he had finished, he pressed his sweaty forehead against hers. "I want to marry you, Mary. I don't want anyone to be able to dispute that you're mine."

"No one will argue with you, Frank."

He pulled her harder against his body. "I don't want to give anyone reason to."

"You really have a buyer for the ranch?" she asked.

"A motivated one. He wants land before winter."

Mary nodded. What was the point of fighting anymore? "I'll make sure not to miss my appointment at the dressmaker's," she said before letting herself out.

Chapter Ten

2016
Matthew

MATTHEW WAS IN TROUBLE.

Big. Big trouble.

He'd known better. When Jess had asked if they could be friends, he'd said yes before he'd thought through the full implications of what being friends with someone he was pretty sure he was falling for meant.

It meant Matthew was still falling, and Jess wasn't.

It meant that the more time Matthew spent with Jess, the stronger the desire to touch her, to kiss her, to back her up to the kitchen counter and wrap her naked legs around his waist became.

It also meant that he was basically powerless to tell her no.

After that afternoon in the attic, meeting there at the end of the workday had become a habit, one that Matthew looked forward to more than he should. He'd ordered her pizza and talked about growing up in a small town near Manhattan. She'd had a client dinner that she'd invited him along on last week, and sure, she'd spent half the time talking about marketing the guy's law firm and the other half discussing shoes with his wife, but Matthew had almost been able to hold the reality of what a relationship with Jess would look like.

Tonight, he'd gone full-on heartsick and brought his banjo. Music had never failed to win women over, only when he emerged into the dusky attic space, he found Jess and a blonde woman already digging into a spread of Chinese food.

The blonde had been laying down on the blanket, her legs propped against the new bed Nell had just placed underneath the bank of windows. She and Jess were laughing about something, but when Matthew entered the room, the blonde had cocked her head to the side and said, "Damn, I'd been hoping you were the ghost."

"Sorry to disappoint." Matthew leaned his banjo against the wall, fighting off his own disappointment.

"Naomi, be nice," Jess said as Naomi flipped so that she was right side up. Sitting on the floor next to Jess, the two looked remarkably similar. Naomi's blonde hair was the main difference between the women, but by their features, they could have been twins. "Matthew, this is my sister, the psychic. Naomi, this is Matthew. He's the contractor."

Matthew offered his hand. Naomi shook with a brisk shake that surprised him, given her willowy figure.

"I'm an intuitive, not a psychic," she said.

"I have no idea what that means, but welcome."

"It means that I can't talk to spirits, but sometimes I sense things. Like you," she looked him up and down, "lack direction."

Matthew's bit back his initial reaction, which was to tell her to mind her own damn business. He didn't want to piss Jess off, even if her sister was a kook. "And do you sense anything here?" Matthew asked as he picked up an untouched carton of beef and broccoli. His favorite.

"I sense that I'm crashing your date," Naomi said with a significant glance toward his banjo case. "Or were you going to serenade the ghosts?"

An unwelcome blush crept over Matthew's cheeks. Naomi was officially unnerving. "Your sister didn't believe me when I said I used to be in a bluegrass band, so I brought proof."

Naomi looked between Jess and Matthew before casting a skeptical glance at Jess.

"What?" Jess asked. "How many people do you really know who play the banjo besides Steve Martin?"

Naomi shrugged, conceding the point. "Do you sing?"

He did, but he hadn't been planning to share that much. He hadn't sung since his brother-in-law had passed. They'd been in the band together when they were younger. Matthew had sung and played the banjo. Rob had played the fiddle. They'd had two other high school friends to do the guitar and the drums. The band hadn't lasted past their second year at K-State, but Matthew and Rob had played together at family gatherings every now and then.

"Right then," Naomi snatched an egg roll in one hand and her coat in the other. "You two have fun. Just make sure you snuff the lights before you get naked, otherwise the whole neighborhood will get a show." She looked Matthew up and down from the doorway to the stairs. "Unless you're into that."

When he got up the courage to meet her eyes Jess's face was as scarlet as his felt. "You told your sister about the footsteps."

She swiped a piece of tofu off the top of a pile of noodles with her chopsticks as she avoided looking him in the eye. "I wanted her professional opinion."

"And?"

"Yours were the only footsteps we heard after they guys left."

Matthew nodded. They'd heard the footsteps two weeks ago. She'd been teasing him about his musical past while he'd finished off their pizza. They'd heard the same progression as the last two times. The disembodied sound of heavy boots across the floor, followed by the light, almost frantic ones running across the attic space. Then nothing.

They'd waited in fruitless silence for half an hour afterward—well, not entirely fruitless, Jess had fastened herself to his arm and basically not let go until they'd had to get into separate cars.

"You look nice," she said.

He looked down. He wore an old hoodie and jeans with even older sneakers. Matthew hadn't wanted to look like he thought this was a date, but he'd gone home and showered the dirt and dust off of him. His hair wasn't quite dry.

"Well, cleaner than normal, anyway," she said. Then stole a piece of broccoli off the top of his container.

"I didn't mean to run off your sister."

"Eh," Jess took a swig from a can of beer. "She had to go pick up Oscar so Rachel could go to work anyway. I just didn't want to be here by myself after dark. You want a beer?"

"Please." Jess opened a can of a brand he didn't recognize and passed it to him. "So who are Oscar and Rachel?"

Jess swiped another piece of broccoli before settling back against the bed. "Her roommate, roommate's kid. It's a long story, but basically they are platonic life partners."

"Maybe you can tell me the story sometime." Matthew was trying not to sound too hopeful.

Jess's gaze was already on his banjo. "Maybe after you show off your musical prowess."

Matthew hadn't played for anyone but himself in a long time, and the only other times he'd played for a woman, it had been a ploy to push them into his bed. This was a new sort of intimacy that Matthew wasn't sure how to navigate. The words "platonic life partners" echoed through his brain where his good sense should be living. Is that what was in his future with Jess? Were they going to continue to develop this connection without ever exploring the kind of relationship he wanted to have?

As he chewed another bite, Matthew understood where he was, but he had no idea what Jess was thinking. For the moment, she was watching him expectantly, but he knew she'd been hurt, possibly gaslit, in her last relationship, so he didn't want to push her. But there would only be so much of being friends with her that he could take before this arrangement became unhealthy for him too.

Jess made a hurry-up motion with her hand, and Matthew couldn't help his grin. "Give me a minute, woman. I just spent the whole day building your house. I'm starving."

The indignant choking sounds Jess had made upon being called "woman" made it entirely worth it. Jess's eyes flashed as she said, "That is so not how this is going to go."

If this had been a date, Matthew would have asked her exactly how she thought things should go. At the same time, he would have been clearing space on the blanket and taking her beer out of her hand so he could maneuver her onto her back. But since this wasn't a date, Matthew took another bite and let his silence speak for him.

Jess showed her defiance by picking up her phone and scrolling, ignoring him completely until Matthew relented and opened his banjo case. He could feel Jess's eyes on him as he fit his picks onto the fingers on his right hand. He settled next to her with his back against the bed, and she rotated so she could watch.

Matthew started with "Foggy Mountain Breakdown," because even if he wasn't planning on sleeping with Jess, he was still trying to impress a girl. That was the whole reason he'd learned the song in the first place. Luckily, the song took so much of his concentration that he didn't have energy to spare to wonder if Jess thought he was the biggest nerd she'd ever met. The fear that she would think he was ridiculous hit him as he played the last two notes.

Only, when Matthew raised his eyes to Jess's, he found her staring at his lips, her own mouth parted, a dazed look on her face. Matthew knew that expression. It sparked the yearning he'd been tamping down the last few weeks. His fingers still recalled how smooth the skin of her cheek had felt beneath them the last time he'd touched her. He set the banjo aside and shifted so he could cup her jaw with the hand that wasn't covered in banjo picks. Her eyes swept to his as she realized that Matthew was going for it.

He was going to kiss her.

Jess wasn't stopping him.

Could she be falling for him too?

A chill breeze ruffled Jess's hair just before Matthew's hand landed on her cheek. Then swift footsteps crossed the attic space. Jess's hand gripped Matthew's arm. Her fingers were so cold, he could feel them through his hoodie. They both startled as the door to the stairwell slammed shut just as the heavy booted footsteps sounded on the stairs.

Two hard knocks rattled the door in its frame when the boots reached the top of the stairs, and a shrill scream rent the air. Both he and Jess covered their ears. When it stopped, the whole attic was still and eerily quiet. No sounds of distant traffic, no neighborhood dogs barking, not even the sound of the wind rattling the old windows.

"What the hell was that?" Jess said, her words coming between pants.

Matthew rubbed at the spot in his chest where it felt like his heart might explode from between his ribs. He shook his head, unable to form words. Despite the unexplainable footsteps, he hadn't taken Jess's ghost idea seriously until that very moment.

"They shut the fucking door," she said.

It was only as warmth crept back into the room that Matthew realized the space heater had kicked back on. He hadn't noticed when it had turned off. The eerie silence dissipated, and along with it, the heaviness faded. The attic felt normal again, rattling windows and all.

"It's not possible," Matthew said.

"What are we going to do?"

"Not stay here," Matthew said, shaking off the stupor enough to start packing up the food.

"I'm not going down that stairwell, are you kidding me?" she said.

Before, Jess had been watching him with admiration. Now there was fear in her beautiful gray eyes. Matthew couldn't help it, the need to soothe her was too strong to resist. He cupped her chin with both hands and said, "I'll go first. I'll make sure you get home safe, okay?"

Jess swallowed, and Matthew could feel the bob of her throat. Then she nodded. "Okay. Let's just get out of here."

It didn't take them long to get out of the house, even less time for Matthew to follow Jess home. Her apartment was downtown, just a few blocks from the house. Matthew's house was across town, and he spent the whole twenty-minute drive white-knuckling his steering wheel. And he might have left his bedside lamp on when he went to sleep that night.

The next day, Jess acted as if nothing had happened, so Matthew followed her lead. She hadn't wanted to hang out in the attic again, though, so Matthew was back to hoping to run into her at the coffee shop. She seemed to be timing her visits around him, though, because she was there almost every time he was over the next few days. That's where he told her about the coffee tasting Anthony had invited him to.

It had barely taken her any cajoling to talk him into bringing her along. Matthew wanted to spend time with her, and even though there hadn't been any more incidents, he also didn't want her anywhere near that attic.

"It's a fantastic business opportunity," Jess said. "He can convince me to carry his coffee in the inn once it's open."

Matthew closed the truck door behind her and circled around the front to the driver's side. He'd picked her up from her apartment for the first time since they'd started hanging out. She lived over a lighting shop downtown in one of those new lofts. He hadn't seen much of the inside, but what he had seen looked expensive. It reinforced his idea that Jess far outclassed him. He wondered what she'd think of his tiny two-bedroom house. His used furniture. The lack of decoration. The profusion of bookshelves.

He'd never been tempted to hire a designer before, but he was suddenly desperate to bring Nell in to make him look like less of a lazy slob in the off chance Jess ever saw the inside of his house. Though that would probably never happen.

They were pretending that the ghosts had never happened, but they were also pretending that the almost kiss had never happened either, and that was more difficult for Matthew to ignore. Especially with the way she'd clasped his elbow as she tramped down the sidewalk in her high-heeled boots on the way to his truck.

Matthew had wanted that kiss. He wanted her with a vehemence that wasn't going to fade as long as he kept seeking her out at every opportunity. Distance. Separation. Those were the only things that were going to allow his feelings for Jess to dissipate, but he didn't think he was strong enough to let go.

Jess

JESS HAD MADE A COMPLETE fool of herself to be able to tag along with Matthew to his friend's house. She'd made up some bullshit about making business connections with local establishments and wanting to know more about coffee. She had been talking out her ass. They both knew that, but she was excited that Matthew had brought her along anyway. Jess had grown so accustomed to spending Thursday nights with him that the idea of going home by herself, even if she had plenty at home to keep her occupied, left her feeling empty.

Emptiness with regards to Matthew's absence wasn't something she had let herself contemplate much yet. Jess just knew that if Matthew was going somewhere, she wanted to go with him. And the renovations would be done in the next few weeks. If she didn't take the time to establish a regular friendship now, Matthew would move on to a new job and their fledgling connection would fade like a wisp of smoke from a snuffed candle.

Jess didn't want that. She wanted them to keep burning.

It had absolutely nothing to do with how, when Matthew had come with her to her client dinner a couple weeks ago, looking like an English professor in his corduroy sport coat with elbow patches, she'd wanted to cuddle up against him just to feel the rough fabric on her skin. His hair had been clean, his red baseball cap nowhere to be seen, and she'd wanted to push her fingers through the red-brown waves. He hadn't shaved all week, and his stubble was almost a beard. Jess kept catching herself staring at the place where the coarse hair framed his lips and wondering what that contrast would feel like against her skin.

He wasn't wearing a sport coat this week, but he did have on a clean flannel and a pair of Chucks she'd never seen him in before.

"You were going to carry his coffee anyway," Matthew said as he slid into the driver's seat.

"True," Jess said. "But he doesn't have to know that. For all he knows, I'm coffee clueless. You're putting us in contact, being a pal."

"Right. A pal." Jess didn't miss the flash of hurt that crossed his face as he flipped the ignition, but it was gone when he turned her way to check traffic. She wanted to tell him not to be hurt. Not to lose patience or give up on his crush. That she was almost there. Then she tamped those thoughts so far down, she wouldn't even remember she'd had them in a few minutes. There was no way she was ready for another relationship. Not now, maybe not ever. She was cool with spinsterhood.

"Have you ever been to a cupping before?"

She shook her head. "Nope. Never."

"Expect Anthony to ask you if you taste cherry or orange or tobacco or something in specific cups. I find it easiest to agree, since he's only looking for confirmation. If you disagree and say you taste vanilla when he wants blueberries, he'll argue with you about it the rest of the night."

"Sounds like fun." Jess grinned. "So, like, I can just pick my favorite muffin flavor or soap scent and pretend I taste it in the coffee."

"Don't," Matthew said.

"Cinnamon Crunch."

"Jess."

"Cedarwood and eucalyptus."

"Stop."

He was saying stop, but his mouth was twitching and his eyes shone in the passing streetlights, so she kept going.

"Whiskey and amber?"

"All right. It's your funeral. Don't say I didn't warn you."

"Sandalwood and elderberry. You want me to keep going?"

"You are evil, you know that."

Jess let out a low laugh. "Oh, you have no idea."

Matthew rolled his eyes and ignored her.

The tasting was even more pretentious than Jess thought it was going to be, but that didn't mean she didn't have fun. She didn't really argue with Anthony about the flavors in his coffee, mostly because she wanted to make a good impression because he was Matthew's friend, but she did confess that she didn't always taste what he was after. Instead of putting him on the defensive, it launched him into a treatise on the variety of the bean and how where it was grown at what altitude and how it was dried all contributed to the flavor, not just the roasting.

Anthony's wife, Gigi, gave her a knowing smile and offered Jess a beer while her husband continued his lecture.

"So how long have you two been dating?" Gigi asked when Anthony had cleared the coffee away and Gigi had placed two large pizzas on the table instead.

Jess reached for a slice and took a huge bite, leaving Matthew to answer. She didn't trust herself to speak on the topic. She was equally likely to confess her budding feelings for Matthew or to lie and make up long, sordid romantic past for them.

"We're just friends," he said.

Anthony huffed a disbelieving chuckle into his beer. Gigi crossed her arms as she leaned against the table and said, "Uh-huh. How did you meet?"

"He's my contractor," Jess said as she swallowed her bite of veggie pizza and elbowed Matthew in the ribs. "My friend Nell and I are in the process of renovating this abandoned Victorian house into an inn—well, it's a B&B, but my partner won that coin toss, so we're calling it an 'inn.' Matthew's overseeing all the work."

"You're the B&B girl?" Anthony said, his eyebrows raised in surprise.

Out of the corner of her eye, Jess saw Matthew shake his head ever so slightly, but pretended she didn't.

"That's actually why I talked Matthew into bringing me tonight. We're going to hire someone to run the place eventually, but all of our applicants have been lousy so far, so I'm starting to hunt out supply contracts to get us started. We can't serve breakfast without coffee, and I'm so not interested in going the Folger's route."

Anthony cringed. "Thank God."

He fished out a business card and told Jess who to call at his office to start working out a contract. Then he looked between Matthew and Jess, made eye contact with his wife, and said to Jess, "So are you sure you two are just friends? Because you look like maybe you've got that friends-with-benefits thing going on."

Matthew choked on his beer, and Jess patted him on the back as she felt her cheeks burn. "We're just friends," she said, ignoring how saying it out loud while she was touching Matthew felt like a lie, because Jess was aware of the electricity flowing between them the same way it seemed Anthony was. "Seriously," she said when the couple still looked skeptical. "This is the most we've ever touched."

Anthony and Gigi both looked to Matthew, who was still wheezing into his napkin, but nodded his agreement.

Jess couldn't handle the awkwardness, so she grabbed another slice of pizza and said, "So Matthew tells me you just got back from Costa Rica," and Anthony barely let anyone get a word in for the next hour.

On the drive back to Jess's apartment, Matthew was silent. It was not a companionable silence. It was heavy, latent, filled with words Jess could tell he didn't know how to say. She wasn't sure if she had the fortitude to tease him out of it; she hadn't been sleeping well since that night in the attic, so she watched the streetlights pass her window.

When he parked in front of her building, Matthew made no move to get out and get her door like he'd done earlier, so she unbuckled her seatbelt and faced him, her back resting on her cold window, her heart pounding.

Before she could speak, he said "I'm not sure I can do this anymore" into the steering wheel.

"Do what?"

"Be your friend."

"Matthew—"

He held up a hand and faced her. "I don't want to just be your friend. I never have. I've tried but—"

Before she knew what she was doing, Jess launched herself across the gear shift and wrapped her arms around Matthew's neck. "Shut up," she said, and just as he lowered his hands to encircle her waist, she dropped her lips to his and kissed him like she'd been dying to for weeks.

Matthew's hands tightened around her waist. With her knees in the passenger seat, Jess pressed her chest into him. He ran his tongue over her lower lip, and she opened for him. His tongue swept against hers, seeking, asking. She licked into his mouth, and his hesitancy fell away, replaced with bare, burning want. Heat ignited inside her, and she met him stroke for stroke as his hands worked under her shirt to grip the bare skin over her waist, and Jess half straddled him between the gear shift and the steering wheel. She ran one hand down the skin of his neck between his hairline and behind the collar of his shirt.

"Come inside," she said in the breath between kisses.

"I can't," he breathed back, but made no motion to stop what they were doing.

"Please?" Jess slid all the way over onto his lap.

"I can't," he said again, this time pulling his head back into the headrest so he could look her in the eye.

Jess gave him a flirty smile and braced her hands on his shoulders as she ground against the bulge in his jeans. His hands tightened on her waist.

"Sure you can," she said. "It'll be easy and fun."

"Jess," he pushed her hair back from her face and cupped her chin. It was Jess's favorite thing he did, and she wanted him to do it every day. Then he took a deep breath, and said, "I can't be your rebound."

Jess jerked back into the steering wheel.

"What?"

"If I were to come inside, it would mean something to me. More to me than to you, and as much as I'd like to be, I can't be your plaything."

His eyes were on the dash as he spoke, but that was probably for the best. It was hard to insult someone to their face.

"That's what you think this is?" Jess asked as she shifted back into the passenger seat and fished her purse out of the footwell. "That I think you're some kind of toy?" She tried to hide the hurt and shame she was feeling, but she knew her voice quaked and her limbs shook with repressed rage.

"Jess," he said as his hand landed on her back.

She slapped it away. "Don't touch me."

"Jess, come on," he said again. His tone scolded, as if she were overreacting.

It took her two tries to get the truck door open, and Matthew sat there, watching her rising panic as her need to get away from him turned frantic. When the door finally cracked open, cold December air rushed in.

"Jess, I didn't mean..."

Her boots hit the ground and she swiveled on her heels to face him. "Yes, you did."

Then Jess ran, crossing the street by dodging between the slow-moving cars of Christmas shoppers. Matthew followed more cautiously, waiting for the light, but he was still on the street, shouting her name as she searched for her keys in her oversized purse. Metal glinted in shadow, and Jess had never been so thankful to live above a lighting store.

"Jess!" Matthew's call was closer. "Jess! Jessica, please."

He was on the curb when she turned around, keys in hand, and she fought the tears gathering in her eyes. "Go home, Matthew."

"Jess, I'm sorry."

"Me too." She didn't trust herself to say anything more and let herself in the plexiglass door that led to the lofts above the lighting shop. He jogged the twenty feet between the curb and her door. She met his eyes as he approached. She saw the penitence mixed with shock in his expression, like he hadn't realized his words would be offensive.

Jess was so done with people telling her how she felt or how she should feel or what her relationships meant to her. She locked the deadbolt just as his hand landed on the handle, then ran up the stairs, leaving him to bang ineffectually on the door below.

Chapter Eleven

1908
Mary

LETTIE WAS THE DRESSMAKER'S name.

Mary had never known. She still made her own clothes with the fabric Wolfgang brought home after the cattle drive. She hadn't needed anything new in the last year. Moving to town had been the perfect excuse to wear all the fancy dresses she'd made with the supplies Wolf had always spoiled her with. Mary sometimes missed the simple clothes she'd worn on the farm. The old soft dress she wore when she worked in the garden was nearly in tatters, but it had always been her favorite, and it was buried at the bottom of her trunk. She hadn't dared unpack it lest Edie take it upon herself to turn it into rags.

It was also possible that Mary had been living so much inside her head over the last few months that she had already met the woman who was currently taking her measurements. She couldn't be that much older than Mary was, and yet she seemed to be running this whole business by herself. Lettie certainly seemed familiar with who Mary was. Though the whole town knew who Frank was. He made sure he was involved with everything.

121

"I've never told you how much I like your dresses," Lettie said from where she measured between Mary's shoulders.

"Oh. Thank you," Mary said. "Sewing has always been my favorite part of the day, even if there were days back when I was living in the country where I was so tired, I could barely see my stitching by the time I got around to it."

Lettie let out a quiet laugh. "I can't count how many times I've fallen asleep with a lamp still burning and sewing in my lap. It's downright dangerous."

"My husband used to say I was going to ruin my eyesight trying to sew by firelight." Mary caught the smile on her lips as she remembered Wolfgang scolding her, then trying to cajole her into going to bed with him. Then she remembered she was standing in a dress shop being fitted for her wedding dress to another man. "My late husband, I mean."

Lettie squeezed Mary's shoulders. "I met him a few times, I think. He was tall and didn't speak English very well."

A brittle, reluctant smiled graced Mary's lips. "He barely spoke English at all when we were first married. We never needed words to communicate." It had been months since Mary had let herself think about those early days of their marriage, when they'd orbited around each other during the day, each speaking their own language, but coming together so completely once the sun went down. She missed the way they'd come to trust one another with their vulnerabilities. How they'd slowly learned each other's languages the way they'd learned each other's hearts and bodies. Mary blushed as she remembered Wolf's leanly muscled chest. "I could almost understand him when he left for the cattle drive."

She added a chuckle at the end that she didn't feel. Lettie gave one of her own. "He bought you fabric," she said. "And dress patterns, before he—" Lettie bit off her words.

"Disappeared?" Mary supplied.

"Yes." She circled around Mary so she was facing her. "He seemed eager to get back to you. I know that doesn't fix that he never made it home, but he meant to come home to you."

Mary knew that Wolfgang would never abandon her. That only death would keep him from her. It almost broke her heart all over again to know that he had set out for home and never made it to her.

"Thank you," Mary said to Lettie anyway, because Mary knew she meant well.

"He seemed kind," Lettie said, tugging at her own sleeves.

"He was."

They shared another sad smile, then Lettie said, "But if you're going to get married again, Mr. Black certainly is the catch of the town." She motioned for Mary to follow her toward the bolts of fabric she had piled on a worktable, and Lettie's words fell flat on the floor between them like the platitudes they were.

As Lettie showed Mary the beautiful cream-colored sheer cottons that were the season's favorites, Mary couldn't stop thinking about how much she didn't want to marry Frank. It wasn't that she just wasn't ready to remarry after Wolfgang. It was that Mary didn't want anybody but Wolfgang. She'd found distraction with Frank, some of the healing she needed to deal with her grief, but she didn't want to marry him. Maybe didn't even want to continue seeing him.

For the first time since she'd come to town, Mary wanted to go back home to the ranch. She could live there on her own. She could learn to manage the cattle with help from her friends there. Mary could keep up her kitchen garden, could help Josephina, the preacher's wife, deliver babies. That was the life she wanted. Not this sitting, city idleness that gave her little choice but to swim in her own restless heartache.

Even with all of those thoughts squeezing her chest in guilt, Mary went through the motions of picking out fabrics and allowing Lettie to dream up the most extravagant dress she could. Let her earn a decent commission from this wedding dress; one of them should get something good out of it.

Chapter Twelve

2016
Matthew

IT HAD BEEN A WEEK since Jess had run away from him. He didn't blame her. He should have realized that when she started kissing him, it was because she returned his feelings, not because she was looking to use him for comfort and gratification. He'd hoped they'd been building a connection, but the emphasis on their friendship that night with Anthony and Gigi had made him doubt. Then Anthony had had to go and bring up the whole "friends-with-benefits" subject, and all Matthew's surety that Jess had feelings for him had flown out the window.

For a minute, he'd thought a friends-with-benefits arrangement sounded like heaven. As the dinner had worn on, Matthew had played out that scenario in his mind, and there was only one way that ended. With him hopelessly forever in love with a woman who wasn't sure she wanted him. Better to walk away before that even happened.

Matthew had run the words over and over in his mind on the drive to her place from Anthony's. He'd wanted to tell her he couldn't just be her friend anymore. It was too hard when he was falling in love with her, and he'd wanted to tell her that if she couldn't love him back, he needed to know so he could go back to just being her contractor. They'd be done working on the house by February, and then they'd never have to see each other again.

But she hadn't let him get that far.

She had kissed him before he'd worked up the nerve to ever utter a word. Jess's lips on his had been like ascending to heaven. Like crashing through the firmament and soaring on clouds while a choir of angels sang backup vocals to the heated exaltations of his desire.

He'd wanted to go inside with her. Hell, if he could have figured out how to get both their jeans down far enough with her sandwiched between him and the steering wheel, he could have taken her right there in the truck. He'd kicked himself a million times since last Thursday for assuming. Because Matthew had known that Jess wore her cheerful sarcasm like a shield. She still hiding so much hurt, still finding her footing after her last relationship. There wasn't any way to go back and do things differently, but he wanted to tell Jess he understood why she'd reacted the way she had. He wanted to tell her that she didn't have to hide from him. That he saw her pain, turmoil, and that little kernel of hope she clung to like a lifeline, and he wanted all of it.

First, though, Matthew had to figure out how to get her to talk to him again. Then he could tell her he hadn't been defining their relationship for her, just clumsily expressing his own needs.

He'd stopped what he was doing multiple times to rub his hands over his face and chastise himself over how he'd bungled it all as he remembered the way she'd gone from soft and pliant to stiff and cold, like she'd frozen on the spot.

And then she had literally run away from him. She'd locked that deadbolt right in front of him, and then she'd locked him out completely. She'd ghosted the construction site. The weekly update on her blog about the renovation had been side-by-side progress shots instead of anything new. She hadn't been at the coffee shop, though he still checked twice a day, just in case.

What was worse was that Jess hadn't answered any of his phone calls. The only text she had answered had been Tuesday afternoon. Matthew had stopped by the coffee shop on his way to Dana's. When Jess hadn't been there, the desperation to see her, to hold her and tell her that he was hers, that he had been since that day she'd told him off for being late for a meeting he hadn't been late for. He'd shot off a quick text while he was waiting in line.

Please, let's just talk about this.

Her response had been immediate, and clear enough.

Whatever was going on between us is over. Leave it alone.

What Jess meant was that she wanted him to leave *her* alone.

So he had—while berating himself thoroughly for screwing up so completely. Matthew had tried telling himself it was for the best. That he needed to spend his spare time on planning promotions for his book, which was being published in March.

It wasn't lost on him that this was something he could have used Jess's help with.

He'd been tempted to ask her more than once if she had any pointers but had decided against it because that would mean exposing that secret part of his life that only Dana knew about. And if he told Jess about his books, about how he didn't understand Facebook or Twitter and the idea of starting a blog made his hands shake with anxiety, she'd learn about a part of him that he wasn't comfortable sharing with anyone. And what if she read the book? What if she found out about Clarissa?

There were days when he regretted ever attempting publication. He wasn't cut out to be a public figure. He was an introvert who enjoyed making things. Marketing, business. Those were what Rob had been good at.

Grief had nearly knocked him off his feet at the thought of his friend. That happened sometimes, Matthew would remember how much Rob was missing. Not just how the manuscripts he'd encourage Matthew to query were now being published, but Jackson's growth spurt, the way he still couldn't pronounce his *R*s. Rob would have fallen in love with Dana all over again if he could have been around to witness her resilience. Matthew was impressed with her daily. He thought she was dealing better with the changes in their lives than he was, though he knew her pain must be fathomless.

Strangely, it was remembering his sister's courage that gave Matthew one last course of action to try with Jess. It terrified him, and when Nell arrived with her beefy personal trainer fiancé a few days before Christmas, Matthew's heart beat so hard, he was convinced Nell could see it through his shirt.

He let her show her fiancé around at first. She'd brought him in to show off where they had started painting and papering the guestroom walls with the wallpaper she'd spent weeks agonizing over. When she came back downstairs, Matthew pulled her aside to go over the holiday schedule and get her approval on a couple of last-minute decisions. She'd reminded him about the arbor he'd agreed to build for her wedding, even though the wedding wasn't until May, and they made a whole other appointment to discuss the design just so he could ask her what he really wanted to know.

"Have you heard from Jess this week?"

Nell went from her usual brand of bright and bubbly to cold and stiff as she dropped her smile to purse her lips. She levelled Matthew with her narrowed eyes, but she said nothing.

Not wanting to seem like he was completely hopeless, he said, "She mentioned something last week about taking some more pictures before Christmas."

Nell's expression narrowed further, and Matthew knew she saw right through him. "She's with her folks for the holidays."

Jess's family lived on the other side of Kansas City, in a small town in Missouri. It was about a two-hour drive from Topeka, and Matthew knew all of that because Jess had told him. Before. When they'd still been friends. He'd also known she'd planned to spend a few days with them over the holidays, but Christmas was still more than a week off.

Jess had told him that she and her mom were close, so maybe she'd gone early just because she missed her mom. Matthew couldn't deny that she'd had a hard year. He just hoped that it hadn't been his fuckup that had sent her running home.

"Oh" was all he said aloud.

Nell nodded, and the movement of her head along with her crossed arms said everything she didn't need to say. *She was trying to get away from you, you monumental asshole.*

Matthew swallowed. He wanted to explain, to fall to his knees and plead with Nell to tell Jess that he hadn't realized he'd had that kind of power. He wanted to tell her that he was a bumbling fool of a man whose insecurities hadn't let him believe that the most perfect woman he'd ever met could possibly have feelings for him. But he was also strangely thankful that Jess had someone to defend her so fiercely, even if it made Matthew the bad guy.

Instead of saying any of that, he took a deep breath and said, "I got her a Christmas present. Could you get it to her?"

He hadn't really bought her anything. Dana had. She'd only met Jess the once, but anyone who would play with Jackson for an hour straight without complaining about it later was a winner in his sister's book. It probably didn't hurt that when he was over at Dana's, he couldn't make himself shut up about Jess. Three days ago, his sister, knowing he never thought about Christmas until the day before, handed him a gift bag and told him he owed her sixty bucks and naming rights for his first-born child.

Matthew had been confused until he looked inside the gift bag. A long, chunky gray scarf with buttons on one side pooled onto his lap. He had no idea how it worked, but he had no doubt that Jess would. And that she would love it.

Matthew had been carrying it around in his truck in hopes of running into Jess at the job site. Obviously, that wasn't going to happen.

He hadn't expected Nell to uncross her arms or for her scowl to release her lips into neutrality, but she sounded reluctantly impressed as she said, "Get it to me, and I'll get it to her."

"It's in the truck."

Nell sighed and made an impatient shooing motion.

Matthew jogged out to the car and grabbed the bag. What he hadn't told anyone else was that he'd included an advanced copy of his book. His original idea had been to send one to her business through his agent, but this was better, more personal. It allowed him to sign the book, to write Jess a note that bared everything.

It probably wouldn't work. Jess would probably think he was a fool and never even look at him again, but he'd had to try something.

As soon as he handed the bag to Nell, Matthew wished he could have taken it back. The book, the inscription. It was too much. The scarf would have been more than enough.

Jess

THE STREET WAS STILL as she let herself into her apartment the day after New Year's. It had snowed overnight, and the thin blanket of snow had been left mostly undisturbed at this early morning hour. Jess smiled at the snow-covered awnings lining the avenue, knowing that in a couple of hours, the shopkeepers would tramp in and open shop, and a couple hours after that, the civil employees would all be out to lunch, the first day back after the holiday. Life would resume as it should for Jess too. She would do yoga, shower, go to the coffee shop, and get back to work, but first, she would have this quiet, chilly morning all to herself.

As much as she loved her family, Jess's mom's house never ceased to be a spectacle. Even on Christmas, her mother had invited half the women from the shelter she ran, and they all did goat yoga in the barn while her dad put the finishing touches on Christmas dinner. Yeah, her parent's house was now a place you could go to do goat yoga. Jess had been skeptical when her mother had brought it up a few months ago, but Jess could admit when she was wrong. It was hilarious. Laughing at a kid staking its claim on her sister's backside until she fell out of three-legged-dog had been the best Christmas present Jess had received.

Jess hadn't realized how much she'd needed to talk to someone about everything that had been going on. But when she'd run to Blue Springs after Matthew had rejected her, her mother had listened to her story. About Ana, about the ghosts, about whatever was going on with Matthew.

The best part of having an adult relationship with her mother was that they'd figured out how to listen to one another over the years. The comments Jess had used to take as criticisms she could now see for the observations they were, and her mother had learned how to give Jess enough space to process the observations instead of pushing her to talk before she was ready.

It hadn't been until New Year's Eve, when it was just the four of them hanging out at the kitchen island, eating Chex mix and drinking champagne, that her mother had asked, "Have you spoken to Matthew since you've been here?"

Jess had flipped a bagel chip on the tile countertop and shrugged. "I asked him to leave me alone."

"And do you think that was the right decision?"

"For the moment, I need space to figure out how I feel."

"But you knew how you felt before he challenged the sincerity of your feelings for him?"

This was where Jess still had to work to not get upset, because Jess hadn't necessarily wanted to talk about why what Matthew had said had upset her so much.

"I was apprehensive, but cautiously optimistic."

"And the only reason you're not speaking to him is because you thought he was telling you how you felt, like Ana used to do."

"Right."

"And it has nothing to do with him being the first man you've had real feelings for?"

Jess's forehead had *thunk*ed onto the countertop. She shook her head as her hair fell around her in a current of curls that she hoped would wash her away from this conversation. The hair fort was perfect place for hiding from the world and from her feelings and from telling her mom that she had landed on the exact heart of the problem. Outside her lingering insecurities, Jess didn't know how to be in a relationship with a man. And her mom so was not going to let it rest. So she might as well face it. Damn it.

"I guess I never saw myself ending up with a guy," Jess said as she flipped her hair back and sat up. "I always thought that when I found my forever person, it would be a woman." Swallowing a sip of her champagne almost choked her because her heart beat so fast. She'd barely let herself think the words, let alone say them out loud.

She did not, however, miss the look of triumph in her mother's eyes.

"You do know it doesn't make you any less queer if you fall in love with a dude, right?" This was from Naomi, who had been chatting with her father, the source of the sister's entrepreneurial spirit, about her upcoming online membership community launch.

"I know," Jess said, but her voice was smaller and meeker than it should have been.

Because she was beginning to feel like no matter what she did, her sexuality still wasn't going to be defined on her terms.

"How do you do it?" Jess asked Naomi. "How do you hang on to your identity?"

Her sister knocked back the last of her champagne and held her glass out to their mother for a refill. "By not defining myself by other people's judgments of me. You should give it a try."

Their mother had shot Naomi a stern look then, but Jess had been thinking hard about the idea for the last two days. Could she really separate her identity from how others perceived her? How much of the way she behaved had always been performative of who she wanted people to think she was and how she actually behaved?

She'd certainly felt freer lately, more Jess than she had in a long time. So that was a good start.

Inside her apartment, everything was quiet and cold. Jess turned the heat back up and flipped on the space heater she kept in the living room. While the house warmed up, she browsed through her accumulated mail. Nell had been collecting it for her while she was gone. There were also two Christmas presents under the tree she'd positioned in the living room window, a blue bag and a shiny red one. The blue one was from Nell, a gift card to her favorite day spa and an earthy-scented set of candles called "namaste." Jess set them on her coffee table and lit all three pillars so the scent would mingle with the warming air, and thanked her cousin for wishing her peace and calm after her chaotic year.

Now all she had to do was figure out what to do about Matthew.

Where he got the idea that she was fucking with his emotions, she had no idea. Sure, they hadn't really discussed anything, but they were getting to know each other, laying the groundwork for a relationship—at least that's what she had been doing. He had apparently been wallowing in being friend-zoned and had misread her kissing him when she did as a way to manipulate him rather than to stop a conversation that didn't need to be had.

Maybe she hadn't been as up-front with her feelings for him as she could have been. But she'd barely been able to admit them to herself, let alone tell him what she wanted. She'd had no idea other than he was the only person she'd wanted to spend time with, and her definition of "time with" had expanded to include "time while naked." She knew that now that she was back in town.

None of that changed how his presumption and rejection had hurt her, and how his claim that she was using him as her rebound had her doubting her judgement in people so monumentally that it had been good to be around her family and their ridiculousness. They'd made crowns out of fake holly and baked gingerbread and Naomi had burned a yule log and given Jess a protective charm she was supposed to wear under her clothes. She needed more of her family's particular brand of zany. It had been years since she'd spent more than a day or two with them at a time, and that was one thing Jess was going to change in the coming year.

Jess assumed the red bag was also a gift from Nell since it had no tag and no card. Jess pulled out a chunky scarf that could also be worn as a cowl. It was super squishy and according to the tag, handmade out of a wool/alpaca blend of yarn. She snuggled the scarf up to her nose and inhaled. The faint whiff of lanolin lingered on the fabric, her favorite part about wearing wool. The other object that had been in the bag was a book. It had a black cover with silver lettering. It had the words "advance reader copy" stamped across the top, which she'd never seen before. It was only after she'd examined the title, *The Black Alley*, that she noticed the author's name was Matt Zimmerman.

Matt Zimmerman. As in her Matthew?

She sat up straighter and flipped the book jacket open, looking for the author bio. *Matt Zimmerman, born 1980, lives in Topeka, KS where he works as a contractor by day and crafts murder mysteries by night...*

Jess closed the book. Matthew wrote books? Why had he never told her?

Curious, she whipped out her phone and looked him up on Amazon. She found out that this was the first book of a series, and that it was his first published novel. It wasn't due to be published for a couple of months, so this must have been the copy his publishing house had sent him.

She sat on her floor the whole time she had allotted for yoga, tracing the letters of his name on the cover. What did it mean that he had sent her his book? And the scarf? Was he trying to make nice? Apologize? Make up?

Jess looked again for a note or a card, shaking out the scarf, holding the gift bag upside down. It wasn't until she flipped through the book checking to make sure nothing was stuck between the pages that she saw the inscription on the title page.

I love you. I screwed up. I'm sorry. with his name signed below, only recognizable as his because she knew his signature. It only now struck her as being the typically illegible author's scrawl.

Jess sat staring at his name for a long time, trying to wrap her mind around the idea that Matthew loved her.

Chapter Thirteen

Jess

SHE WAITED UNTIL FOUR o'clock to drive to the jobsite. All of Jess's plans for yoga and getting back to work had fallen by the wayside. She'd sat reading on her living room floor most of the day, only stopping around two when she realized her bladder was ready to burst and her stomach was cramping for lack of food. Her head ached from having forgotten to feed her caffeine addiction.

The only food she had in her house was some spoiled orange juice, some moldy bread, and a jar of peanut butter. A shower, some aspirin, and two spoonfuls of peanut butter later, she was on her way to the jobsite with a fresh cup of coffee. Her plan was to show up just as they were shutting down for the day.

Jess half hoped Matthew would already be gone so she could put off their confrontation for a while longer. It had already been two weeks, what was a few more days? Her luck didn't hold. Matthew's faded red truck was parked right out front. Jess took a deep breath, tucked the book under her arm, and marched up the front steps.

In the three weeks since Jess had been there, the whole house had transformed. The walls had been finished and painted, the wood floor was being prepped for finishing, and Cal was setting up at a sawhorse table in the dining room painting the trim that went around the window seat white.

"Hey, Jess," he called as she passed by. "Matt's upstairs."

"Thanks," she said. "The place is really looking great."

Cal beamed as if he'd done the whole thing himself.

She found Matthew in one of the back bedrooms, on his hands and knees, apparently inspecting the newly refinished floors.

Jess hadn't known what she was going to say to him, only that she needed to talk to him, but now that she saw him, gorgeous ass in the air, checking for gaps between the trim and the floor, she found the words.

"What the hell is this?" she asked, more venom in her voice than she knew she was feeling until she said it, waving his book in the air.

Matthew jumped to his feet. "Jess! You're back."

"Damn right, I'm back. Now, care to explain?"

He looked back and forth between the book and her face a couple of times. "How much have you read?"

Jess opened the book and flipped to about three quarters of the way through and glared at him. "I'm this far."

He flinched. "It's not her."

"I know it's not her. It's the electrician. Interesting character, though."

"She's not you."

"Of course she's not me," Jess said, closing the book and dropping it on the floor in front of her. "Give me some credit.

You had to have written this at least two years ago. No, I'm more interested in what it says about you that you think you're in love with a woman who looks just like the teasing bitch of a character you wrote."

Matthew stared at her, standing so still, Jess thought he might be afraid to move. "So, you're still upset with me then?"

"Dammit, Matthew, I don't even know what to think right now. I've spent the last two weeks convincing myself that you probably didn't think I was a manipulative harpy, that it was just a misunderstanding, and coming to terms with how I feel, but then you give me a book that has a character who looks exactly like me, who behaves exactly the way I was afraid you thought I did, and then on the title page, you tell me that you love me. I'm starting to think you like torturing me."

"I just wanted you to speak to me again."

"Did you even mean that?" she asked, toeing the book's spine.

He took one step forward, gauging her reaction. When she only glared, he took another and another until all that was between them was the book on the floor.

"Of course I meant it." His voice, which had been strained and tight since she'd come in, softened into tenderness. He picked the book up and held it back out to her. "And it has nothing at all to do with Clarissa."

"Nothing?"

"Aside from the fact you know without a doubt that you are more beautiful than any woman I could ever conceive of."

"Right."

Jess took the book back, but she wasn't convinced. It must have shown on her face, because Matthew kept his distance, watching her warily.

"The attic is nearly finished," he said. "Would you like to see?"

They had decided to keep the attic as its own studio apartment, either for the manager they had yet to hire or to rent out as a luxury room to guests. The giant bank of windows in the nook where the bed fit had made it Jess's favorite room in the whole house until the door-slamming incident. Jess hadn't been back in there since, but it was still daylight, and she was curious. Jess nodded and tucked the book back in her bag before following Matthew up the back stairs.

She could tell Nell had been there, because a new oriental rug covered the floor in the living area and the bed had a brand-new white duvet.

The whole thing had been painted. The ugly indoor/outdoor carpeting in the living area had been removed and the original hardwood floors refinished.

The mustard-yellow cabinets and Formica countertops had been ripped out and replaced by white floating shelves and new butcher-block counters. The spots where the range and refrigerator should be were still empty, but Nell had already been emailing her ideas. Most Jess had rejected because they were outrageously expensive professional models. Nell was having trouble remembering their budget and not getting swept away with her ultimate design fantasies.

"Cozy," Jess said, sitting on the edge of the bed. She bounced a couple of times to test out the mattress.

Matthew stared out the window over the sink on the opposite side of the apartment.

Jess wanted to know what he was thinking. As if somehow knowing what he was feeling would help her know what she was feeling. Right now, Jess had no clue. Exhaustion overwhelmed her, and she lay back in the bed, attempting to sort out her emotions as all her conversations from her vacation mixed with everything the book and being in the same room with Matthew had stirred up.

She was pissed, but she couldn't decipher if she was mad at him for the book stunt or if she was just angry that he'd thought she was using him in the first place. She had missed him so much in the last two weeks that she almost physically ached with it. She was horny and lonely, and she wanted to be more than somebody's muse. Jess wanted him to think of her as his forever person, but she pushed that desire out as implausible. They didn't know each other well enough for that yet.

"Why didn't you tell me that you're a writer?" she asked finally, looking up at the ceiling.

She heard the wood creak under his feet as he crossed the room, then felt the bed sag as he sat, then laid down beside her.

"I was embarrassed."

"Because of Clarissa?" Jess rolled her head to find him already watching her.

He nodded. "And because it's a private part of me. Only Dana and Anthony know that I do it."

"Oh yeah, you are gonna sell a ton of books."

He grinned, and Jess felt a giggle rise in her throat that she hadn't expected. She shouldn't be so easily disarmed, not with everything she'd been feeling, but she couldn't get enough of his stupid, handsome face.

Matthew reached out and brushed a stray curl out of her face, and Jess remembered the first time he'd tried that, and how she'd been creeped out by it. Had he been surprised to see one of his characters walk off the page and right into one of his job sites?

"You're wearing my scarf," he said.

"It's cute, and I was cold," Jess said.

"It looks good on you."

Jess didn't want to blush, but she felt her cheeks heat anyway. His smile had vanished when she met his eyes again. His hat was sitting crooked on his head because of the angle of the bill to the bed. She tugged it off. Then she came up on her elbows to smooth his hair.

Matthew closed his eyes, sighing, and Jess continued running her fingers through the hair that looked more red than brown in the weak late-afternoon sun.

"I missed you," he said and opened his eyes. A hand came to her cheek and caressed, just like it had the last time they'd been in this room together.

Jess, with her fingers still in his hair, lowered her gaze from his hairline down to his eyes. The tender way he was looking at her sent a chill down her spine.

"I'm sorry," he said. "I never meant to hurt you."

Jess leaned into the hand that cupped her cheek. "I'm sorry I was a coward who couldn't admit how much I liked you."

"You were trying to let your actions speak."

"But you needed words."

Matthew pushed himself up onto his elbow and brushed his lips against Jess's, then pulled back to make sure that was okay.

Jess latched onto him much the way she had done the first time they kissed, but this time, Matthew wrapped his arms around her too, shifting her so that she was mostly beneath him on the bed. His chest was heavy and hard against hers. His breath came in pants between kisses, and he tasted like tobacco and nicotine.

Jess laughed against his lips.

"What's funny?"

"You told me you didn't smoke." And he had. One day when she'd arrived, every other member of his crew had been standing in a circle taking a break, not all of them smoking, but most of them. Matthew had been the only one inside still working.

"Anymore. I said I didn't smoke anymore."

Jess giggled again and pressed up into him, nipping at his bottom lip, eliciting a groan from deep in his chest. "Had a bit of a relapse did you?"

Matthew let a little more of his weight settle over her and Jess wrapped her leg around his to hold him there.

"Well someone I know had me near panic with worry because she wouldn't return my calls."

"I'm sorry."

Jess kissed down his jaw and up to his ear as his free hand traced down her side then found its way under her under her sweater and along the top of her jeans. She rose into his touch, trying to coax his fingers toward her fly and down.

"Matthew," she said, already begging.

He answered with a groan that was almost a growl, dipping his fingers below her waistline. He had had just skimmed the edge of her panties when he stilled.

At first Jess was confused and asked him why he'd stopped, but Matthew shushed her. That's when Jess heard it too, footsteps on the interior stairs. Booted feet on hardwood creaked steadily toward them.

Together they raced to their feet, straightening clothes and smoothing hair. Matthew had just gotten his hat back on when the footsteps reached the top of the stairs, and no one was there.

MATTHEW WAS GOING TO fire whoever was coming up the stairs. He didn't care who it was or why they were looking for him. He didn't care if the damn building was on fire, he'd been on top of Jess, on the bed, the only thing stopping him from worshipping her completely were the clothes he hadn't had a chance to remove yet.

Now his heart was pounding for a different reason. They had scrambled to their feet like teenagers afraid to get caught by their parents. He had done it because the fact that he was still on the jobsite, about to bed one of his employers, hit him as soon as he heard the footsteps on the stairs. There was no reason why he couldn't pursue a relationship with Jess, but maybe having sex with workers still on site was crossing a line.

Jess waited for whoever it was to cross the threshold with a guilty look on her face, ensuring that whoever it was would know he'd been about to feel her up. But the footsteps stopped, and no one came. Jess peered around the corner of the living area and into the stairwell. Matthew did the same, placing a hand on her waist, ready to pull her back in case the door slammed again. The hair on the back of his neck stood on end, but nothing else happened. There was no second set of footsteps, no screaming.

"There's no one there," Jess said.

"I know," he said. Striding forward to the stairwell, he descended the stairs and scanned the hallway, seeing no signs of anyone on the second floor. There were still men downstairs, packing up and getting ready to leave, but there was no way one of them could have made it down there and out of sight before he'd come down. There hadn't been time.

Matthew ran back to the attic, where Jess still stood by the bed, pale and gripping the painted white metal post.

"Anyone?" she asked.

He shook his head.

"You guys haven't had anything strange going on, have you? Noticed anything since the last time?"

He shook his head again.

Jess was scared. He could see it on her face, in her eyes as they darted from the stairwell to him to the closet door the boogey man might hop out of.

"I think we should go downstairs."

Jess nodded and took his hand as he turned again toward the stairwell, like she was afraid to even go near it. She held his hand as they descended to the first floor, where only Cal and Steve were left, finishing up the last piece of trim before they left for the day.

Jess dropped his hand as they entered the dining room and examined the hinged bench on the newly completed window seat.

"Did anyone go upstairs just now?" Matthew asked Cal.

"Everyone else left fifteen minutes ago," Cal said. "Unless they came up the fire escape to the attic."

"I thought I heard footsteps in the hall," Matthew said. "Must have been you guys."

"It was probably just old Randy," Steve said, concentrating on filling a crevice in the molding with white paint.

"Randy?" Matthew asked. Jess turned around now, done feigning indifference.

"The ghost that walks around up in the attic," Steve said, like Matthew should know what he was talking about. "How have you not heard Randy?"

"Why hasn't anyone told me you've been hearing somebody up in the attic?" Matthew's temper was flaring into his voice. He prided himself on being a pretty mellow guy most of the time, but he'd thought he and Jess had been the only ones experiencing things.

"Because there's never anybody there," Cal chimed in. "Man, I can't believe we've been here for months and you haven't heard Randy before tonight." Matthew didn't correct him. The guys didn't know he'd been meeting Jess in the attic after-hours or hanging out with her.

"He's down on the first floor all the time," Steven said. "Hardly ever upstairs."

"Why do you call him Randy?" Jess asked.

The guys looked to each other, then to Matthew, as if just realizing Jess was there. They exchanged glances that communicated that they knew exactly why Jess had been upstairs alone with him for so long. So maybe they had an inkling about him and Jess.

"The theory goes," Cal said, "That the ghost is on his way upstairs to visit a lady friend, and since we hear him two, three times a day, we figure he's a pretty amorous guy. . ."

"I get it," Jess said. Then, looking at Matthew she said, "I've got to get going."

Matthew had to stay to lock up until Cal and Steve were done since the foreman had gone already, so he said, "I'll walk you out."

Neither of them said anything on their way to her car, though they joined hands automatically once they were out of the house.

"If I hadn't been hearing them myself, I'd tell you not to take their story too seriously. They make up stories like that about every house, but this time . . ."

"My sister thinks I need to do some research into what this house has been through, then do a blessing before we open up. Unless we try to market ourselves as The Haunted Inn. 'Come get spooks with your scones.'"

Matthew grinned and pulled her into his arms. "Sounds delicious." Then he kissed her, his lips moving slowly, languidly over hers, a contrast to the two frenzied kisses they'd shared so far. The idea had been to remind Jess of how charged they'd become upstairs, but keep control, only the more he kissed her, the more he wanted to lay her out over the hood of the car.

"Can I see you tomorrow?" he asked.

"Meet me for coffee?"

Matthew bent down to kiss her nose. He'd never really noticed how much shorter she was than him before, but standing so close, she barely reached his collarbone. "I want to cook you dinner."

She looked like she had questions, but all she said was, "That would be nice."

He gave her one last soft kiss, then stood in the street until she'd driven away. When he looked back at the house, it was to find Steve and Cal staring at him from the porch.

"Don't say anything," Matthew said as he passed them to lock up.

But as he made his way inside to check the back door, he could have sworn he heard Cal tell Steve to pay up.

Chapter Fourteen

Jess

NELL BROUGHT JESS A dinner of Thai take-out while they went over resumes for the inn manager. Nell had been fielding reservations for their April opening, which they were already booking up. But both of them had underestimated how long it would take to find a qualified hotelier to run their new little venture. Jess had a feeling she was going to be stuck changing sheets soon while Nell wouldn't stop talking about how she refused to spend her honeymoon anywhere but a beach, like Jess was the one holding them back, not the lack of qualified applicants.

When the resumes had been sorted into "interview" and "reject" piles, Jess sat back in her chair and got around to what she really wanted to talk about. Feigning nonchalance, she picked at the last of her noodles in the carton and asked, "Have you heard any rumors about a ghost at the house?"

"What?" An amused, and maybe even excited, smile crept over Nell's lips. "No. Dish!"

Jess explained about the first time she and Matthew heard footsteps on the stairs to the attic. "We blamed it on squirrels at the time, I think because we didn't know each other, and neither of us wanted the other to think we were crazy, but we were up there with Jackson a couple months ago and heard it again. I felt something rush past me, and it freaked me out but then Matthew touched my face—"

Nell squealed and bounced in her chair. "You didn't tell me you let Matthew touch you before the truck kiss. How was it, did he cup your cheek? Or run his finger over your jaw? Ooo, or did he touch your hair?"

Heat flooded Jess's cheeks. "I mean, he sort of cupped my jaw and ran his thumb over my cheek."

Nell squealed again, and Jess flinched, the pitch was so high.

"Why didn't you tell me?"

"Matthew touching me like that short-circuited my brain so hard that I forgot about potential ghosts."

"Would you forget about the ghosts for a minute? Was that when you realized you were into him?" Nell was nodding, like she understood all of Jess's motivations, and maybe, despite Jess's best efforts to keep everyone at arm's length, Nell had managed to weasel her way in closer than her standard

"I mean, maybe I had an inkling after that. I think I mostly just realized that I could trust him with me, you know?"

Nell fluttered her fingers over her heart. "Ugh, see, I knew you two would get along, and you obviously got his Christmas gift, so tell me, what was it? What happened between you two, and what does it have to do with ghosts?"

Jess's hand landed on her scarf before she realized it, and Nell's eyes examined the garment more closely. Jess had enough scarves to never wear one more than once a season. But not only were they seriously cute, her shoulders and neck were almost always cold, so Jess acquiring a new scarf was nothing new to Nell. Jess wearing a scarf that someone else had picked out for her had never happened before.

"He got you this?" Nell's hand landed on the knitted fabric that was draped over Jess's shoulder and squeezed. "Ooo, it's so soft! He did good."

The blush that had just started to fade from Jess's cheeks intensified again as she raised her own hand to caress the fabric. It was soft and fluffy and warm and everything she loved about winter scarves. Basically, it was perfect.

"Yeah, he did."

Nell sat back and sipped from her green tea. "Okay, I want to gush about whatever is going on between you and our adorable contractor, but I seriously need to know about these ghosts. You heard footsteps again?"

"Right. So we were up in the attic—"

Nell squealed again. "We?"

Jess was not going to play along. "Yeah, Matthew and me."

"You were alone in the attic?"

"Yes, but—"

"How's the new bed?"

Jess bit her lip, and her entire face burned.

"Oh my God, is that what you were doing when you heard the footsteps? Please, please, please, tell me you were having make-up sex."

Jess sighed. "No, we were in the attic *making out* when we thought one of the guys was gonna catch us horizontal with Matthew's hand down my pants."

"Whoa," Nell said.

"Yes," Jess nodded. "Anyway, there was—"

"Was this like the prelude to make-up sex or more like angry foreplay?" Nell asked.

"It can't be make-up sex if we've never been together before."

"How am I supposed to know that?" Nell asked. "All I know is that you took off because he hurt your feelings the night you two went out to that coffee tasting, and it was so horrible you didn't want to talk about it. What happened, by the way?"

Jess rolled her eyes and retrieved the book from the breakfast bar where she'd finished reading it over a cup of coffee in the couple of hours between her return from the house and when Nell showed up with dinner. She had been right. It was the electrician.

"Read this," she said, holding it out to her friend. "Read the whole thing, and then we can talk about what happened, and where Matthew and I are now."

Nell looked at Jess like she was crazy, but took the book and began to open it without even glancing at the cover.

"Not right now," Jess said, and Nell tossed the book on the floor with a "Fine, tell me about this ghost then."

Jess told her what had happened in the attic the last two times she and Matthew had been alone together and how the crew had been hearing footsteps too. "We can't have guests getting scared off by disembodied footsteps."

"I don't know," Nell said. "Maybe we could make it into a thing. Be 'the little haunted inn.' We were worried about attracting people year-round. Maybe this is how."

"I thought about that. It would gain a ton of attention, but is that who really want to be? The Haunted Inn?"

Nell tapped her lip as she thought about it. "It's not the same clientele we were planning to target."

"Exactly." Despite what she had said about Matthew frying her brain with his touch, Jess actually had put in a lot of thought in as to whether to play up the possibility of a ghost on her blog, and she'd ultimately decided against it.

"But we'd probably be able to charge more," Nell said, perking up to the idea.

"It feels smarmy to me. Like, what if it is ghosts, and they're suffering, and we're profiting off their suffering? It would be wrong." It had been something Naomi had said over Christmas when Jess had told her about the door-slamming incident.

The light that had sprung into Nell's eyes at the idea of having a larger operating budget snuffed itself out. "I'd never thought of it that way before."

"Yeah" was all Jess could say.

They sat in silence for a few minutes, contemplating the implications of what they were dealing with.

"I think I'm going to do some research this week and see what I can find out about the history of the house. I don't remember the realtor mentioning anything about deaths on the property or it being haunted, do you?"

Nell's brows crinkled. "No. I don't. She should have though, if someone knew of it, you're supposed to have to disclose that sort of information—I think."

"Maybe she didn't know?" Jess offered. The house had been abandoned for decades. They'd purchased it for a steal from an investor who'd had it for ten years and hadn't done anything with it. For the first time, Jess wondered if he hadn't followed through with the flip he'd had planned for it because of the footsteps.

Nell shrugged. "Maybe." Then she picked up the book again. "You really want me to read this?"

Jess nodded. "Every. Single. Page."

Nell tossed it into her bag with barely a look. She obviously hadn't noticed the author's name yet. "The things I will do for gossip." She nailed Jess with an accusatory glare. "This had better be worth it."

Jess grinned just thinking of the moment when Nell would read the title page.

Matthew

MATTHEW SAT WITH DANA in her home office the next morning, going over paperwork while Jackson played with giant Legos not-so-quietly over in the corner. They'd been there an hour talking about invoices and supply companies and prospective new clients for when the inn was completed. Matthew didn't have a lot of patience for those kind of details on his best days, but this morning, the only thing he could concentrate on was Jess. More specifically, that Jess was coming over to his house tonight. He'd offered to cook her dinner, but his mind was fast-forwarding past dinner to the part of the evening when Jess was relaxed and well-fed and how he'd pull her onto the sofa, situate her against his shoulder, with his arm wrapped around her waist, and take his time exploring the crook of her neck with his lips, and then—

Matthew shook his head to banish the thoughts. If he kept thinking, he'd get aroused, and that was not something he wanted to deal with around his sister.

"You okay?" Dana asked. "You seem spacier than usual today."

"What's the best thing I cook, do you think?" he asked. "Is it the spaghetti?"

Dana snorted. "Hardly."

"You don't like my spaghetti?"

"No," she said, switching her attention back to the stack of files on her desk.

"What's wrong with it?"

"You mean besides the fact that it doesn't taste like anything and you always undercook the noodles?"

"I do not." Dana sent him a skeptical look, and he saw his mom looking back at him. "It's called al dente."

"It's called crunchy. And it's gross. Why are you asking me?"

Matthew shrugged. "No reason."

Dana's skeptical look turned suspicious. "Were you planning on cooking for us tonight?"

"I was planning on cooking for me. I should eat better than I do, you know."

"You're such a liar," Dana said. "Who's the girl?"

Matthew shrugged, but knew it was useless trying to play innocent, so he went for casual instead. Leaning back in the spare kitchen chair he was sitting in, with his legs stretched long and his fingers crossed behind his neck, he said, "Same girl."

"Jess?"

Matthew grunted.

"I thought she wasn't speaking to you."

"She wasn't. Now she is."

Dana raised her eyebrows, trying to stifle a smile. "And you're making her dinner?"

"It sounded romantic when I asked."

"It sounded like a cheap ploy to get her alone with you at your house, but I'm guessing she's game if she agreed. God knows why. Does she know you can't cook? You didn't tell her that you could, did you?"

"I cook," he said. It was true. He fed himself. He didn't live off take out. Sure, he made burgers and eggs and frozen vegetables a lot, but that was still cooking.

"You make good pancakes," Dana said. "You should make her breakfast." Then Dana launched straight back into the discussion about the new lumber company they'd been having when he'd interrupted her. Matthew only half listened as he made a mental list of the groceries he would need and tried to think of any last-minute cleaning he should do before Jess arrived.

Matthew lived in a little two-bedroom house in an old neighborhood that bordered a historic neighborhood with sprawling Victorians like the one Jess and Nell were remodeling. He loved the gigantic old homes, but not for himself, he didn't need much space.

Matthew's house was neat. Almost minimal—not a curated minimalism like the look of so many new remodels he did; he just didn't have a lot of stuff. Most of his money went back into the business. The one improvement he'd made in his tiny house was to cover one wall of his living room with custom-built bookshelves. They were jam packed with all the books he'd collected over the course of his life. Some of his college writing books, some of the books he'd used to learn business and construction, a few biographies, but most of it was his vast collection of mass-market mysteries and thrillers. Matthew had made a study of the genre long before he'd decided to write in it.

Matthew had always loved the way a mystery could evoke a visceral response in his body. His heart would thud during the suspenseful scenes, his brain would churn when different suspects were speaking on the page, and when the culprit was caught and the plot revealed, his sense of accomplishment and relief were as tangible as if he'd been working right along with the investigator in the book. Reading had become, if not an addiction, then definitely a preoccupation. There were books on those shelves that he'd read six times over, just to make sure he hadn't missed a single nuance.

It was only natural that he'd started writing books of his own. It's where his mind went when he was working, when he was driving, when he was basically doing anything that wasn't writing. It wasn't something he'd ever been able to turn off. It was no wonder Jess and Dana had called him spacey.

As he tidied up before Jess's arrival, Matthew found himself wishing he'd done more to make his house homey. He had a decent sofa, a big TV that he never used, and there were a few family photos spread around, but no real decoration. He didn't even have any houseplants. Except for the books, he realized, looking around in the few minutes he had left before he expected Jess, his house was a little bit drab.

It was probably too much to hope that she wouldn't notice.

But hopefully he could lure her into the kitchen with the smell of bacon and pour her mimosas and make her pancakes and she'd be distracted enough by him that his complete lack of style wouldn't matter.

The thought of his style had him ducking into the bathroom to check his reflection in the mirror. He'd washed his hair, so it wasn't as flat as usual. It was still too long, brushing his collar in back and curling around his chin in front if he let the locks fall forward, but he'd managed to comb it back in a way that felt intentional. And his shirt was clean. He'd even ironed it. He only had three nice shirts, and he'd never worn this one before. He'd always gravitated more toward blue or white when he had to dress up. He'd never known what to do with this slate gray one that Dana had purchased for him. But it had called to him from his closet earlier. What better way to encourage Jess's attention than to wear her favorite color? At least he assumed it was her favorite color. Matthew realized he didn't know for sure what Jess's favorite anything was. Just because she was always wearing something gray or black or white didn't mean they were her favorite. Her favorite color could be sunflower yellow for all he knew.

But he didn't have time to obsess over it. Jess was due in any minute. He made sure he hadn't stained his shirt or the one pair of jeans he owned that didn't have holes in them yet. Matthew swiped his palms over the rough fabric covering his thighs.

Jesus, why was he so nervous?

"Because you told her you love her, and you haven't been in a relationship in a decade, you idiot."

He'd actually said it out loud to himself as the doorbell chimed. Good, at least he didn't have any more time to psych himself out.

Jess smiled when he opened the door for her and shoved a bottle of wine into his hands as she pushed past him into the living room. "I wasn't sure what we were having, but that's my favorite wine, which is probably good for you to know if we're going to be a thing. I'm picky about wine."

She drummed her black fingernails against her thighs as she turned in a circle, taking in his home. A smile inched over Matthew's lips as she took a step toward the wall of books. She was just as nervous as he was. That helped.

He looked down at the bottle of wine. Nothing on the label made any sense to him, but he would remember the picture of the cicada. Maybe he'd take a photo of the bottle when she wasn't looking so he didn't get it wrong in the future.

"So, do you do anything *but* read?" she asked, her voice coming from the far corner of the room, one of his favorite books already in her hands.

"I didn't used to. Now I spend more time writing my own books."

She smiled when he set the bottle of wine on the coffee table and joined her in the corner. "That's right. How's book two coming?"

His fingers were brushing that stubborn coil of curls out of her eyes before he had anything to say about it. His feet stepped closer to her until there was barely any space between them. Jess looked up at him with sparkling eyes and tossed the book onto the sofa to her left.

"Book two has been finished for two years," he said, allowing his fingertips to trail down her cheek, along her jaw, and down until he met the soft fluffy fabric of her scarf. "Can I take your coat?"

Jess nodded but didn't move, so Matthew unfastened the top button, conscious of how close his hands were to her breasts. His mind was on the other day in the attic, the softness of her skin, the decadent give of the bed when he'd hovered over her, the scratch of lace against the calluses on his fingertips when he skimmed over the top of her panties.

Was she wearing lace again tonight?

Would she let him find out?

"Um, so, how many books have you written?" Jess asked. Her voice was low, hesitant, like she was afraid to speak.

"I'm finishing up my fourth. And the fifth is due to the publisher in July."

She swallowed as he finished with the bottom button and pushed the gray wool down her shoulders, then flung it over the arm of the couch. "That seems fast. Is it too fast?"

Matthew shrugged. "I have no idea. I'm new to all this." His hands found her waist and pulled her up against him, and Matthew felt like he was breathing for the first time.

Jess tilted her head back; "Oh" was all she said as his fingers cradled the back of her head. Lightning pulsed through him as her long curls tangled around his fingers. He brushed his thumb over the curve of her neck, and she inhaled sharply, then closed her eyes and relaxed against him when he did it a second time.

"Can I kiss you?" he asked.

Jess's fingers fisted into the spot where he probably should have tucked his shirt into his jeans, but now he was thankful she had the fabric to cling to instead.

"Please." Her voice was a whisper over his lips. Matthew felt her plea more than heard it. He slipped his hand beneath the cropped sweater she wore, savoring that feel of silken skin as he brushed his lips over hers in a barely there kiss.

Jess pushed up on her toes, chasing him as he pulled away to meet her eyes. "You are so beautiful," he said.

"Shut up and kiss me." Jess wrapped her arms around his shoulders and pressed down until his lips met hers again.

Had he thought he'd taken his first breath earlier? He'd been mistaken. This was like being born anew. Matthew had never lived before he'd tasted her. Yes, they'd kissed before, but this, with his feelings laid bare, with her having time to accept them for what they were. She still wanted him. She wanted them, and Matthew wanted to get lost in nothing but her. As her tongue circled over his, Matthew could see himself getting lost in them. They were fathomless. Bottomless. They could float in this cloud of desire forever and never find its end.

Jess's hand pressed against his chest, and she pulled away just far enough to rest her forehead against his chin. Her breath came quick, and Matthew's head was still swirling with such yearning for her that he wasn't sure he was still on earth when Jess said, "Is something burning?"

He crashed back into existence as he smelled the acrid scent of burnt bacon and cursed. He'd cooked the bacon on a baking sheet in the oven to leave the stovetop clear for the pancake griddle, and he'd forgotten about it.

"Fuck." He dashed into the kitchen, where the smell was overwhelming. Smoke plumed out of the oven as he opened the door. He pulled the cookie sheet out and threw the whole thing, black bacon-shaped ash and all onto the back porch. He was throwing open the windows when Jess wandered into the kitchen, fanning her hand in front of her face.

"I burned the bacon," Matthew said as he flipped on the ceiling fan.

The January cold bit into his skin through the row of open windows, but the smoke was clearing out of his kitchen little by little. He made a mental note to check the batteries in his smoke detector. The damn thing probably should have gone off.

Jess didn't appear alarmed or startled, just took her time looking around the tiny space. Her eyes snagged on his old enamel diner table. She ran her fingers over the white surface. "I wouldn't have eaten any anyway."

Matthew blinked. "Do you not eat pork?"

Jess snorted. "I don't eat meat."

His hands were running through his hair before Matthew could remind himself that he'd combed it. He was too busy recalling everything she'd eaten when they were together. And yes, now that he thought about, she never had eaten any meat in front of him, but he'd stupidly never noticed before that Jess was a vegetarian. What kind of idiot was he, telling her he was in love with her when he hadn't even noticed such a basic, essential part of her?

"What's your favorite color?" he asked.

Jess blinked. "What?"

Matthew gestured to her outfit, which was a charcoal cropped sweater over gray leggings paired with tall black boots. "I mean, I would have assumed something within the spectrum of what you normally wear, but maybe you like fuchsia or yellow or—"

"Silver gray," Jess said, and Matthew snapped his mouth shut. "My favorite color is silver gray. And I haven't eaten meat since I was twelve and my dad sent my favorite pig to the butcher."

Matthew opened his mouth, then shut it again.

"Yes, we had pigs growing up. And chickens. A donkey. Horses. Dairy goats. Those were my favorite. Mostly we grew vegetables to sell at the farmers' market. That's how I got into marketing, actually." Jess pulled out one of the metal cafe chairs, sat at the table, and pulled her scarf tighter around her shoulders.

The smoke had mostly cleared, and Matthew jumped into action, closing the windows as she spoke. "I made the farm a website as a project in one of my high school classes. I started a blog for it. This was pre-social media. Though I did manage to hook up the website to LiveJournal so it would automatically update there, too, and help grow our audience organically. It helped my mom start selling her goat's milk soap all over the country."

Matthew had snorted at the mention of the ancient blogging platform. "I haven't thought about LiveJournal in years."

Jess crossed her legs. Matthew's eyes traced the curve of her thigh. He couldn't keep himself from imagining the dove-gray panties he suspected her leggings concealed, though part of him hoped she'd surprise him with red lace.

"That's probably for the best," Jess said. "It's pretty rudimentary as far as social websites go. You should see the magic I can work with Facebook these days."

Matthew couldn't help it. He groaned. "God, I fucking can't stand Facebook. Especially since the election. It's political vitriol and ads."

"Well, I'm with you about the politics. I can't with the people fighting all the time, but give me a shot at advertising your books, and then tell me how you feel about Facebook ads."

"I—" Matthew didn't know what to say. "Do you have any experience with books?" That was not the right thing to say, and he knew it.

Only Jess looked amused. She even shrugged. "Give me the weekend. Now, did you have something else planned for our dinner besides charred bacon? Because I am starving."

Her stomach growled as she spoke, and a smile broke over Matthew's lips. She was adorable, and she liked him. This evening was going to turn out just fine.

"Anything else you don't eat?" he asked.

"Turnips, because ew. But as long as there's none of those and no meat, I am pretty easy to please."

"Pancakes? Berries? Eggs?"

"I love breakfast for dinner."

"Mimosa?"

"Oh my god, you might be perfect." Jess said.

"Decide that after you've had my pancakes," Matthew said and turned to the fridge for her drink and the pancake batter.

Chapter Fifteen

Jess

MATTHEW WAS OFFICIALLY the most perfect man she had ever met. He was still a straight man, so of course there were improvements that could be made. Small things. Like he should have tucked his shirt in, and he probably should have had a haircut three months ago. Then again, Jess kind of liked his overgrown hair. She wanted to pull it. Kind of like how she liked his house because it showed off exactly what was important to him. Books. Writing. Comfort.

The place was comfortable, if tiny. The whole house couldn't have been more than a thousand square feet, and that was being generous. The loft she lived in by herself was twice that size.

But he'd poured her a mimosa and turned on his griddle and made her pancakes and eggs and set down a bowl of berries in the middle of the table. She'd eaten half of them by the time the pancakes were ready, along with drinking half a bottle of champagne. But Jess couldn't make herself feel guilty about any of it. She'd missed spending time with Matthew like this over the holidays. When he sat down, he'd offered her the bowl of berries, and when she'd declined, he'd dumped the rest of them over his pancakes. He didn't apologize for finishing them off or make any remarks about how many she'd eaten before he'd even come to the table. It was the kind of interaction she might have had with her family.

As they ate, he told her about his absolute marketing ineptitude, so she gave him a few pointers on how to get started. He still looked completely lost.

"Your agent hasn't given you any guidance?"

"'Open a Twitter account' isn't exactly guidance."

Jess almost choked on her blackberry. "You don't have a Twitter?"

"Should I?"

"Probably about three years ago."

"Right. Well, at least I have Target and Barnes & Noble."

Jess raised her eyebrows. "That is a good start, but if nobody knows your books are available there, you're still just relying on luck."

"So what do you think I should do?" he asked.

Jess licked a glob of maple syrup off her finger, then took a long sip from the mimosa he'd made for her in an orange-juice glass. "Normally, I would suggest that you hire me to be your marketing coach."

"You can't just do my marketing for me?"

"I could help you set up your platform, but all of that is going to hinge on you being your brand."

"No, Tate Fischer is my brand. I'm just the author."

Jess shook her head. "No such thing. You're an artist, just like a painter, an actor, a goddamn YouTuber. You make the product, but the product is not your brand. You're the brand.

The novel, the character, those are all what you sell. Really, your agent should have explained this all to you."

Matthew shoveled an entire egg into his mouth and shook his head. "He's been telling me I'm behind, but he's been giving me a little slack because he also knows I also run my own company."

"Uh-huh. Text me his contact info. I'll call him on Monday."

Matthew choked on his second gigantic bite of scrambled egg. "What?"

"I'll call him on Monday and work out a plan for how to kick your marketing off in time to hype your release at least a little bit. Though you haven't given me much time."

Silver flashed as Matthew's fork twisted between his fingers. "I'm not entirely sure I can afford your services."

Jess rolled her eyes. "Don't be ridiculous. I can't charge you."

He pointed his fork at her. "I should pay you for your work."

"No way."

"Why not?"

Jess held up two fingers. "Two reasons. One, you're so pathetic, I would feel like I'm robbing you blind charging what I normally charge. At least most of my clients understand what it takes to promote themselves. The reason they hire me is because it's worth it to them to *not* do it themselves. Second, it would feel pretty freaking dirty given that I'm planning to take your pants off in about ten minutes."

Jess had been hoping to make Matthew choke again, but instead his fork hit his plate with a clank and a scrape. "You don't have to."

"I want to."

"Yeah?"

"After we were interrupted the other day, I've barely been able to think of anything else."

"Same."

"So, then what are we still sitting here for?" Jess asked.

Matthew wiped his lips with his napkin and stood, plate in hand, then held out his hand for Jess's plate. She offered it to him, and he dumped them both in the sink, not bothering to scrape the unwanted food into the trash or rinse the syrup off. Instead, he led Jess by the hand down a darkened hallway to his bedroom.

It was too dark to make out much of the decor, but Jess wasn't all that interested in what his bedroom looked like as long as he was in it. A soft blue light from the street filtered through his curtains, giving her just enough light to see where his bed was. She backed him up against the mattress and pushed him to sitting and hoped her false bravado hid that she was trembling

Yes, Jess wanted to tear his clothes off, that didn't mean she wasn't fucking terrified.

She kissed him anyway.

He tasted like maple and strawberries, making the kiss more intoxicating than the mimosas she'd had with dinner. Matthew's hand squeezed her waist, then trailed his hands to the swell of her hips, he squeezed there too then reached around to grab her ass. Jess laughed at his groan when he squeezed.

"Why are you so perfect?" he asked.

"You should probably decide that after we've done the dirty," she said against his lips. God, even her voice was shaking. She wasn't going to be afraid. She'd never been afraid of sex before, and she shouldn't be now either. She wouldn't be.

To her surprise, Matthew huffed a laugh against her lips and smacked one ass cheek just hard enough to intrigue her, but not exactly hard enough to sting. She lowered her lips to his jawline, running her chin over his stubble until she reached his neck, then nipped. Not hard enough to leave a mark, but just hard enough to sting, you know, in retribution.

Matthew pulled in a breath through his teeth. "It's like that is it?" he asked, amusement lacing his words.

"You started it."

He pulled her close, crushing her against him. He yanked her scarf off over her head, then ducked his own head to bite her breast through her shirt. A tremor of exhilaration overcame Jess's anxiety, and she didn't know what to do with it. Pleasure reverberated up and down through her bones, bouncing off her toes and frizzing her hair. It had been so long since sex had been about satisfaction, about gratification, about anything other proving her devotion. This delectable thrill with Matthew? It was foreign to her.

Jess allowed her fingernails to zip down his sides, just because she wanted to. The tremor settled into liquid heat between her legs. She wanted—needed—his stupid shirt out of the way so her nails could bite into his skin.

"I am going to tear you apart," she said when he bit down on her other breast, then lathed his tongue over the bite.

"That is exactly what I'm counting on," he whispered.

Jess did what she'd been dying to do for weeks and buried her fingers into his gloriously overlong hair and raked her nails back along his scalp. Matthew tilted his head back into her palms and she devoured him with rough kisses. Bites, sucks, and nips were followed by soothing licks. Jess had never felt like she was going to combust just from kissing before, but if she didn't get Matthew naked soon, she thought it was possible.

He pulled her lower lip between his teeth. Then they were falling backward onto the bed. Matthew rolled so that he was on top of her. Jess heard his shoes hit the floor as he toed them off, though his lips were still battling with hers.

With one last nip, Matthew sat back on his heels and peeled his shirt off over his head, not even bothering with the buttons. Jess wanted to run her hand over the lean, work-hardened muscles she could just make out through the shadows, but he had backed out of her reach.

Matthew lifted first one foot, then the other. He unzipped her boots, then peeled them off her feet and tossed them over her shoulder. Her socks followed, and he kissed his way up the inside of her leg until he reached the juncture of her thighs. Matthew's teeth bit into the flesh just over her clit, and Jess couldn't help the upward motion of her hips. He did it again, and Jess whined.

"This is a good spot then?" he asked, then repeated his bite, adding a quick flick of his tongue. She could feel the moist heat through her leggings, and it was a maddening tease.

"What do you think?" he asked.

"I think we should take these off."

Matthew leaned forward, grasping her waistband in both hands. His chest was finally within her reach and Jess ran her fingers down his shoulder and over his subtle pectoral muscle until she reached his nipple, and pinched.

"Fuck, Jess." His words came out with heavy breaths.

"Stop stalling," she said.

Her leggings were gone in the next second. Then he had backed off the bed, his eyes traveling over her legs and up toward where the thin strip of cloth covered her core. She hadn't worn anything fancy tonight. Just a plain black thong. A black cotton bra, because she hadn't wanted to assume they would end up here. But holy hell, as Matthew's jeans hit the floor, Jess was glad that they had.

"And the briefs," she said, pointing downward with her finger.

Matthew didn't hesitate to slide the dark briefs to the floor, but before Jess had a chance to take in all his naked glory, he'd dived back onto the bed, aiming again for that spot between her legs that made her writhe. This time, he ran his hands up over her hips until he found the straps of her thong and pulled it down her legs.

He paused, kissing his way back up her legs when he got to the crook of her knee. "Have you been tested recently?"

Jess's heart stuttered at the question, so practical in the middle of their lust battle. And just when she'd banished Ana from her thoughts. "After Ana and I broke up. She was sleeping with someone else, but there was nothing."

Matthew angled up her body in what would have been a stellar example of moving from child's pose to plank had they been doing yoga. He captured her lips for a brief kiss. "I'm sorry. I didn't mean to dredge up bad memories."

Jess shook her head and wrapped her legs around his bare waist. "It's an important question. You?"

His left hand slipped under her shirt, pushing the fabric up to expose her stomach, and he levered back to place a kiss to her navel. Jess's legs rested under his arms and all it would take to have his head back between her legs would be for Matthew to duck his shoulders underneath her thighs. In her anticipation for the first stroke of his tongue against her, she almost didn't hear the answer to his question.

"You haven't slept with anyone for a year?"

He shrugged. "I'm an introvert."

"More like a hermit," Jess said, and he chuckled against her belly, then nipped at the sensitive skin where her hip met her thigh, and she screeched.

"I've been writing," he said, then licked the bite.

"Then I suppose I admire your dedication."

Matthew laid kisses over her tummy, moving from right to left until he was kissing down her left thigh until he ducked between her legs in exactly the way she'd wanted him to. He murmured something about determination against her skin, but Jess's brain didn't have time to interpret it, because Matthew's breath fanned over her, and her toes curled with want.

He licked her from slit to clit, then bit her like he'd been doing earlier, and Jess lost the battle. She was at his utter mercy. There was nothing she'd be able to resist from him, and he hadn't even gotten started.

"I have been fantasizing about this for weeks," he said as he parted her folds with his finger.

She hadn't expected him to be all that interested, at least in this act, but Jess was not going to argue with him and tell him that in her experience men were any good at this, because his mouth on her was proving her so monumentally wrong. She'd told herself that she would be cool with this experience when it happened. That she wouldn't be the selfish lover Ana had always accused her of being, but when her hands bunched in Matthew's hair and nudged him just a fraction higher, she couldn't make herself stop.

Matthew was hitting all her sensitive spots at once, like his jaw had been made to pleasure her. And then he slipped one finger inside her, and Jess cursed.

"Too much?" he asked, and started to pull back, but Jess tightened her grip in his hair.

"Fuck no. It's perfect." Matthew gave a satisfied little nip to the inside of her thigh that made her inner muscles pulse. "I'm so close, don't stop."

With another nip to her other thigh, Matthew didn't stop, he pumped his finger inside her while lapping at her clit with his tongue, and Jess felt like a spring coiled too tight, like she might launch into space when the pressure building inside released.

All it took was a crook of Matthew's finger and a bite to the skin over her clit, and Jess was defying gravity, rocketing through the ether until she broke apart amongst the stars. She was nothing but stardust, adrift in a vast universe of pleasure.

Kisses to her thighs and belly brought her safely back down to earth, her body landing before her mind could comprehend that Matthew was kissing his way up her body. When she was fully grounded, she wrapped her fingers around his upper arms and pulled him down on top of her. Maybe she was a selfish lover, because she'd always been turned on by the taste of herself on her partner's lips, and she needed to sample what she and Matthew tasted like together.

He moaned as he fit his body against hers, the hard length of him pressing into her leg. The proof that he had enjoyed pleasuring her as much as she had enjoyed receiving it. "God, Jess." His lips were everywhere, like he couldn't decide what part of her he needed to kiss next, so instead was kissing her everywhere at once. "That was fucking amazing."

Jess couldn't argue with him. It had been a long time since she'd been that uninhibited with a partner. With Ana, she'd always been careful not to appear like she was taking too much, tried to make sure Ana was satisfied, that Ana was assured that Jess had wanted her and only her. All the performing had turned sex into more of a chore than an expression of love. This was something different entirely.

Curious, she reached between them and wrapped her fingers around Matthew's erection. He choked, like he hadn't been expecting her to touch him. She squeezed and he flexed into her touch with a curse. She swiped her thumb over his tip and swept the bead of pre-cum down and pumped. He gave tiny thrusts into her hand like he couldn't help herself.

"I want inside you so bad," he said, his words dazed with desire.

"Yeah, we should do that."

But neither of them stopped what they were doing. Every point of connection felt too good to stop. Then Matthew lowered his head and sucked her right breast into his mouth, sweater, bra, and all, his tongue soaking the fabric. Jess arched into the sensation as her body reset itself, ready for more pleasure. "Dammit, I need to get the rest of these clothes off you."

"And we need a condom," she said, releasing her hold on him.

"Of course," he said, but Jess could tell he'd forgotten.

He pushed her shirt over her head, and Jess wished the lights were on so she could get a proper look at his body, but she was enjoying the intimate isolation of the darkness too much to disturb it.

When her shirt was gone, Jess tamped down her nerves. Her breasts had always made her uncomfortable, and there was no hiding that they were too big for her body now. But Matthew traced the line of her collarbone and over the dark tattoos along her chest that slid to her shoulder and disappeared under her bra, not even glancing at her bra. "What is it?" he asked.

"Constellations in the night sky," she said. "That was my favorite part of living in the country as a kid. I would take a flashlight and my books out behind the barn and read and watch the stars."

"The stars are magnificent in the country." His fingers ran over the patterns she couldn't believe he could see. To her, it just looked like a dark pool of ink on her skin, but his touch was reverent, purposeful, as if he were connecting the dots of each constellation.

Then he traced down the cup of her bra until he found the clasp between her breasts. He had zero comments about her body, he only cocked his head to the side and balanced with his elbows to fiddle with the metal. The release of pressure made the cups of her bra spring loose and exposed both breasts at the same time. Jess felt as if he'd just unleashed two bowling balls, but Matthew didn't seem to notice. All she could make out of him were wide eyes and the flash of teeth as he said, "Well that was magic." Then his mouth was already closing in on her left breast gripping the right between rough fingers.

One of the reasons she was so fond of scarves was that it helped distract from the giant boobs that didn't match the rest of her body. Matthew was oblivious as he lost himself to sucking, nipping, biting, and squeezing.

She hadn't always been fond of having her breasts touched *because* she was so self-conscious about them, but as Matthew groaned against her nipple, she arched into his mouth, feeling the reverberations of each stroke of his tongue as need pooled inside her, stoking her desire with each nip and squeeze.

"Please," she said.

"Please what?" he asked. His voice was rough, lower than she was used to when he spoke, and it was the sexist thing Jess had ever heard, knowing how affected he was from lavishing attention all over her body.

"I need more." Jess didn't have enough vocabulary left to elaborate.

Matthew shifted his hips, and a hard length pressed against her, not seeking entrance, but his offering of more making its presence known.

Jess rocked into him with a curse, and Matthew's lips tightened against her breasts. Jess couldn't help herself, she did it again, even though she knew she was playing with fire. It would be so easy for him to slip inside her from here. And it would feel so good, so natural to just let him have her. But . . .

"I'm not on birth control," she managed to croak out, which had Matthew freezing on top of her.

"Right," he said. "Right."

With a stretch of his long arm, he'd reached over her head and came back with a small box. Jess managed to shimmy out of her bra while he opened the new package, but when he produced a foil pack from inside, Jess took it from his fingers.

She gripped his erection again and stroked just enough for him to shift into her touch and moan, and just when she felt him relax again, she stopped and ripped open the wrapper, then rolled the condom over him.

The darkness made it difficult to see much of anything, but when she looked up, Matthew's eyes were shining as bright as twin stars during the new moon. The light speared right to her heart.

Chapter Sixteen

Matthew

JESS'S SKIN GLOWED like the moon in the dark, the blue hue of streetlights filtered through his curtains just enough to highlight her every dip and curve. Her corkscrew curls sparkled like stars. Her eyes were pools of pure silver starlight as he coaxed her back into the pillows. His lips on her were more tender than the tongue and teeth sort of warring they'd been giving each other so far.

But despite her begging, despite her putting the condom on him herself, Matthew's instincts told him to take this part more slowly, more tenderly than earlier. Not that there was a lack of passion in what they were doing.

Jess's mouth was hot and the slide of her tongue over his made him burn. He kissed her with slow, deliberate purpose. Matthew wanted her to beg for him again. He wanted her to be so far gone with passion that she forgot to be tense. To be afraid.

Matthew was pretty sure she'd thought she hidden it from him, her trepidation, the way she'd basically been trembling until he'd spanked her. They way she'd winced when her breasts had sprung free. He wondered who had hurt so badly that she was afraid to share herself with him.

Sure, this had been her suggestion, but when she'd said she wanted to take his pants off, it had sounded like she'd been daring herself to do it. Pushing herself forward despite her fear. Matthew wanted her to forget her pain, he wanted her to forget to be afraid. Matthew was determined that Jess would get so lost in her pleasure that everything would fall away but the feel of his skin on hers.

It was a triumph when her fingers skimmed over his back, another when her hips rocked up and into his, looking for friction. When she gasped his name between kisses, he knew she was ready. And slowly, so slowly, he guided himself inside her by feel. She tensed at the first press of him into her entrance, but Matthew brushed over the spot just over her clit, the one she'd responded to so well when he'd been going down on her. Her hips bucked up into his, and her body melted beneath his touch.

Matthew kept his thumb in place, massaging slow circles, thrusting in every time he reached the bottom of his circle. It was slow torture, because watching Jess's body build toward orgasm could have brought on his own release. Then add in the compact heat of being inside her, and Matthew was straining for control. Concentrating on her pleasure instead of his own helped, but only marginally.

"Matthew." His name was almost lost in two breathless pants as she reached for him and pulled his mouth onto hers by the hair at the nape of his neck. When his tongue met hers, Jess's body clamped down on his, and the flutter of her inner muscles pulled a curse from his throat the same way it pulled his orgasm from his body: hard and deep and primal. His vision clouded with nothing but pure light until his body collapsed on top of Jess's, and darkness, highlighted by the starshine of Jess's hair against his pillow, slowly filtered back in.

He forced himself up long enough to get rid of the condom, but then joined her back in the bed where she cozied back into him. Matthew had just wrapped his arm around her shoulders, her head settling on his chest when she shuddered in his arms. He'd been about to tell how fucking amazing that had been, but Jess's shudder was followed by a wail and sobs so violent, Jess didn't have the breath to tell him what was wrong.

He was fairly certain it had nothing to do with him, though it wasn't exactly the post-coital glow he'd been looking for; he decided to keep that to himself. He grabbed the box of tissues off the bedside table and gathered Jess in his arms so that he rested against the headboard with her curled up in his lap. Matthew didn't know what else to do but stroke her hair and rub her back until she finally cried herself to sleep.

Chapter Seventeen

1908
Mary

IT HAD BEEN ON A WHIM that Mary had brought Lettie leftovers from the lunch counter one afternoon after she got off. Maybe it had been the conversation about Wolf, or maybe it had just been the companionship of another woman, but Mary had felt more alive, more herself, in that short time while conversing with Lettie than she had in the entire time she'd been in town.

And the food was at least an excuse if Lettie didn't want to be her friend.

The closer the wedding grew, the more Mary contemplated what it would mean to not go through with it. She didn't think Frank deserved to be embarrassed like that, but would it be worse if she called it off now, or simply didn't show up for the ceremony? He would be furious with her either way. There was no getting around that. Anticipating his temper alone would have given Mary pause before marrying him, even if Wolfgang hadn't been in the picture.

As Mary let herself into Lettie's shop that first day, she had been curious to see what Frank's temper might look like fully unleashed. The idea probably should have frightened her, but it didn't. Mary had been living in such a hazy detachment from real life for so long that even something she knew could prove treacherous for her had zero impact on her sense of fear. But she knew it had the potential to make her life miserable.

Perhaps she'd already decided then not to go through with the wedding. Mary couldn't be sure.

Lettie had been confused to see her, but grateful for the food.

"I tend to work through meals these days," Lettie had said as she led Mary into the back of the shop. It turned out that Lettie and her mother ran the shop together. Her parents had started it, but her mother had lost most of her hearing in the wagon accident that had killed Lettie's father. So her mother worked in the back while Lettie saw to the customers in the front and helped with the sewing as much as she could.

"Most nights we sew until the danger of staining the fabric with pricked fingers in the dark is too difficult to ignore."

"You need help," Mary had said.

Lettie had blinked at her. "We are barely keeping up with the workload and with the supply costs. There is no money to hire anyone new."

Mary heard more than Lettie said. They'd likely been struggling even before her father had passed. Now there were fewer hands to help, and being a woman running a business must not be easy.

To distract herself from the way her stomach tightened at the thought, Mary said, "I don't mind helping out in the evenings. I like to sew, and I enjoyed talking with you the other day."

The last bit came out in a little bit of a rush, but a smile had ticked at the side of Lettie's mouth. "I couldn't pay you."

"I wouldn't expect anything other than companionship."

Lettie had picked up an apple out of the basket. "I can give that much." This time Lettie did smile.

For the last two weeks, Mary had spent most evenings with Lettie in the back room of the shop, helping as much as she could. It was nice to not be alone in her room at her uncle's house. To speak to another person her age. To gossip about how the new sheriff, Thomas Wolstone, kept coming round with flowers for Lettie. Those two weeks with Lettie had done more healing for Mary than the whole year since Wolfgang's disappearance. More than any stolen afternoon with Frank, even as she watched her wedding gown grown nearer and nearer to completion each day.

Mary would work on whatever projects Lettie needed help with, but she would not touch the wedding dress.

A week before the wedding was to happen, Lettie was sewing on the final bits of lace around the hem when she caught Mary staring at the dress.

"Are you anxious to see it finished, or do you want to throw it in the fire? I can't tell."

They had spent much of their time together sharing about their childhoods and their pasts. Lettie had let Mary speak of Wolfgang as much as she liked. The other woman always watched Mary with knowing eyes when Mary shared stories of what their life had been like together. How content she'd been with Wolf on the porch, her with her sewing, him with his pipe and his banjo.

"I . . . don't want to give up on the possibility that Wolf is coming back. Not so soon."

Lettie nodded. "I don't blame you. I would wait another year at least if I were you. Hold out for a letter or something."

Mary shook her head even as her soul leaped at the idea of even just a letter from Wolfgang. Would it smell like his pipe tobacco? She could picture his handwriting, the special slanting scrawl of his words across the page. How the letter would begin *Meine Maus* and proceed to tell her all of the adventures he'd been on while working his way home to her.

Mary wanted that letter. She wanted the time to wait for it.

But she knew telling that to Frank would be fruitless. He wouldn't listen to her. He hadn't listened to her.

She shook her head. "Frank won't wait."

Lettie pursed her lips. "Which would you rather have?"

Mary dropped the skirt she was hemming into her lap. The word, "Wolf," felt as if it had been pulled from deep within her very soul and forced out her lips. There was no choice, really. Wolf wasn't there to have, but Mary clung to the elation she would feel upon receiving that letter, on tracing his words and imagining his arms around her once more. It was like having the breath of life circulate through her body, sloughing off this too-long hibernation and remembering what it was like to live.

Truly live.

"Then what do you really have to lose if you were to give up Frank Black?"

Mary took a deep breath. She'd been wondering the same thing herself more and more. But there were things Lettie didn't know. Mary was a widow. It wasn't like she was expected to still be virginal, even if it wasn't exactly proper to admit to one's pre-marital indiscretions. Mary found herself wanting to share with Lettie, so she said, "He insists we must because we have been . . . intimate."

Lettie made an unbecoming noise in the back of her throat. "Funny, that wasn't enough to convince Frank to marry me."

Mary's heart stopped in momentary shock, then broke for Lettie. That Frank had mistreated Lettie in that way made her want to marry him even less.

"Would you still want him if I were to break off the engagement?"

"Ha!" Lettie's laugh was loud and sarcastic. "I'd rather stick this needle in my eye."

Mary cocked her head, intrigued by the vehemence behind the words. And perhaps a little jealousy that Lettie was able to conjure up such a strong conviction. "Why do you say that?"

Lettie studied Mary for a moment, then said, "I don't speak my mind often. I've learned the hard way that most people don't want to hear it, and it can affect business."

"But?" Mary asked.

"But," Lettie gulped in a breath of air, "I also learned the hard way that Frank Black is a cold-hearted bastard who only cares about money."

A startled laugh escaped Mary's throat at the unexpected curse. "What did he do?" she asked, but Mary thought she had an idea.

"He set about seducing me until he found out the dress shop hasn't been profitable since my father died. And then you came to town, land rich and looking to sell, and two weeks after he'd ended our engagement, he was driving you through town, proud as a peacock, as if he didn't notice you weren't anything more than a ghost by his side."

"Oh." Mary twisted her fingers in her lap. "I feel like a ghost sometimes."

"I know, and that man is taking advantage of your grief to get his hands on your money."

"But I don't have any money," Mary said. The sales from both farms had yet to be finalized.

"Yet," Lettie said. "And if he's married to you when you receive it, that money will be his money."

"But I don't want the money."

"What is it you do want?" Lettie asked.

Mary chewed her lower lip. "To go home."

Lettie nodded as if Mary should just do that, as if it wouldn't be heart-wrenching to go back to the ranch without Wolf to come home to. To live there without him.

But as they worked in silence, a scheme began to form in Mary's mind. If she could get her parent's land sold. Could make sure the money was hers and hers alone, she could buy more cattle, hire men to help her keep the ranch in shape. She could replant her vegetable garden, raise more hens. She could go back to the life that she loved and keep the ranch Wolf had loved alive for him. And if he had survived. If he someday made his way back to her, Mary would be there.

"I don't want to give up on Wolf," Mary said. "I know it's irrational of me, that if he were alive, he would be back by now, but it's not just that. I loved the life we had together, not just because it was with him, but because I loved where we lived, what we did. It wouldn't be the same without him but going on this way is beginning to feel wrong. And maybe I don't want to give up on myself either."

A proud smile curled over Lettie's lips in the fading sunlight. "What are you going to do about it, Mary Zimmerman?"

Chapter Eighteen

2017
Jess

IT TOOK A MOMENT UPON waking for Jess to disentangle herself from her dream. In it, she'd been running, she didn't know from what, something that made her heart race and her anxiety spike. But then she'd seen Matthew's faded red ballcap in the distance. She'd changed course, and started running toward him, only she'd never gotten any closer. Until suddenly, he was right in front of her with wide eyes and a surprised expression as she barreled into him.

The fall had woken her, and she clutched the sheets between her fingers until she was certain her world was stable. That was when her senses started to invade her consciousness. She smelled coffee. The sheets between her fingers were slightly crunchy, like they were made of cheap cotton, and she was definitely naked.

A quick physical inventory highlighted the ached between her thighs and the heaviness of her limbs. She also felt the itch in her throat and the crust on her eyes that told her that the image of her sobbing all over Matthew right after he'd given her the best orgasm of her life had not been a dream, but was, indeed, a memory.

Fuck.

Why couldn't that have been part of her dream?

There was no way this was going to end well. Who even did stuff like that?

"Thanks for the amazing sex, don't mind me, I'm just going to indulge in a minor breakdown."

Why had she even done that?

Jess wasn't exactly sure except that she had been feeling too much. She'd been elated and devastated all at once, and it didn't make any sense because Matthew was perfect, and the sex had been so out-of-this-world, and there was no way he'd want to do that again with her when all his hard work was met with a sobbing, snotty mess.

She was just glad he was already up. At least he wasn't lying there next to her, looking at her with expectant eyes. Was it too much to ask that he was in the shower so she'd be able to sneak out without having to face him and explain herself?

With one last self-pitying stretch, Jess pulled on her clothes from the day before, though she hadn't been able to find her panties. Whatever, they weren't one of her nice pairs.

But when Jess tiptoed past the bathroom, the door was open, the room dark. She doubled back, because her bladder was bursting, and took the opportunity to splash water over face and scrub the mascara rings from underneath her eyes. Her eyes were still puffy from crying, but at least she no longer looked like a demented raccoon.

She would have gone straight to the front door and let herself out, but she'd left her bag looped over the back of the kitchen chair, and from jazz music drifting down the hall and the clink of dishes, that was exactly where Matthew was.

And good god, the man wasn't wearing a shirt. Did he not realize it was freezing? But as he pulled a mug from the cabinet and poured it full of steaming hot coffee, he didn't seem to notice the chill. He pulled another mug from the cabinet, pushing a few out of his way until he found a silver-gray one. Jess's heart melted a little bit when he filled it with coffee then topped it off with a dollop of cream, just how she liked it.

Maybe she hadn't insulted his masculinity and scared him off after all?

She couldn't be certain. To be fair, Jess was pretty sure her mind had stopped working altogether as she'd watch the play of his lean muscles under his skin. He was even more beautiful in the daylight.

The toaster popped, and Jess jumped. Matthew shot her a sly smile that let her know he'd known she was standing there the entire time as he pulled two strawberry Pop Tarts from the toaster and onto a plate.

"Pop Tart?" he asked.

Despite her trepidation, a laugh jumped from Jess's throat. "Have you been talking to Nell?"

Matthew shook his head, "Not about you."

"Then how did you know?" she said as he took both the plate of Pop Tarts and the mug of coffee from his hands and took a seat at the table.

"Know what?"

"That these are my favorite treat."

"I didn't." Matthew shrugged and popped two more into the toaster. "I keep them around to bribe Jackson with, and since I used up my cooking repertoire on dinner last night, I improvised breakfast."

Jess smiled to herself as she broke off a corner of crust and dunked it into her coffee. "I knew I liked that kid."

Matthew pulled a chair around so that he sat facing her, his elbows on his knees, his coffee mug cradled in his palms, his long torso still distractingly bare, all topped with a concerned frown.

"About last night," he said.

Jess's heart sank. So they weren't going to pretend nothing weird had happened. Damn it.

"Did I hurt you?" he asked.

Jess shook her head, her bottom lip clenched between her teeth.

Matthew nodded as if he didn't quite believe her. "Because if anything I did or said anything that contributed to—"

"No, it wasn't you."

His eyes were so sincere, so grieved on her behalf, that Jess was ashamed of herself for wanting to escape. How shitty would it have been of her to leave him with this guilt and worry? Not when none of it had been about him.

"You were amazing," she said. The memory of having him inside her in the dark washed over her, leaving a shiver in its wake. "Fantastic, actually."

There was that self-satisfied smile she would have expected to see this morning had she not bawled all over him like baby. It looked good on him. Matthew deserved that smile.

"I was . . ." Jess didn't know what word to use to describe why she'd burst into tears. She wasn't entirely certain herself. "Overwhelmed, I guess."

Matthew pushed her frizzy curls out of her eyes. "It was all the orgasms, wasn't it? Too many?"

Jess batted his hand away. His grin was back, and she ran her thumb down the stubble on his cheek. She liked it when he smiled at her. No one had looked at her like that in so long, so openly admiring, like she mattered to them for being her and not for what she could do for them.

"I am still dealing with a lot of hang-ups left over from Ana." Jess raised her eyes from where her thumb traced Matthew's lip and met his sad gaze. As if he could see each wound without Jess having to tell him what they were. She could see the plea for her to let him help heal them spilling from him, like a cup brimming over.

Jess yearned to let him, wishing that dbe enough.

"One of them is wrapping my head around how it's not a betrayal to be with a man, to even want to be a with a man."

The care in Matthew's eyes remained, but he clenched his jaw and spoke through his teeth when he said, "You don't owe her anything anymore."

"Up here," Jess tapped her temple, "I know that, but here," she tapped her chest, "years of self-censoring 'bisexual' into 'lesbian' doesn't just go away overnight."

Matthew covered the hand that was at her heart with his own. "I'm not really sure how to help with that, except to say that I'm yours. For as long as you'll have me. No conditions."

How in the world was she supposed to say no to that? He was only offering her the only thing she had ever wanted from a partner. "God, why are you so perfect?"

"This is where I remind you that I just screwed up so badly that you left the state and wouldn't return my texts for three weeks."

Jess raised Matthew's fingers to his lips, recalling the conversation with her mother over Christmas. "I can recognize why you thought you needed to protect yourself."

"Weren't you doing the same thing?" he asked.

Jess shrugged. Probably she was. "I have an appointment with a therapist next week, someone my mom recommended. To talk about how manipulated and gaslit I felt by the time I asked Ana to move out."

A muscle in Matthew's jaw flexed again, "It'll be difficult to convince me that Ana isn't a manipulative gaslighter."

"What she is or isn't is not the point."

"You're right." He ran his hand through his still disheveled hair, and Jess couldn't deny her physical attraction toward this man. He was magnificent. "I just don't want us to be one of the things that upsets you."

"We're new, but I like us. I was afraid I'd upset you."

"I'd only be upset if I'd scared you off."

Jess sat back in her chair and picked up her Pop Tart before it got cold. "Good, then you won't be freaked out when I start a ghost investigation at the house."

Maybe she had to duck out of the way to avoid being sprayed with Matthew's coffee when he choked, but the fact that she felt free to laugh at him instead fear that she'd be yelled at for the mess, was completely worth it.

Chapter Nineteen

Matthew

JESS HAD NOT BEEN KIDDING about her ghost investigation. She'd spent the last week finding out who'd owned the house and looking for police records of anything tragic having happened in the area. She'd even spent two whole evenings away from Matthew at the library sifting through microfiche of century-old newspapers in case any of the old homeowners' names came up in the headlines. Matthew hadn't minded too much, because he was still on a deadline for the end of the month, but he'd wished she could have done her research in the armchair in his office. That way he could have taken her to bed with him afterwards.

When he'd texted her goodnight the night before, she'd responded by asking him when the best time to bring the psychic by would be.

His response of *Never* had been ignored.

Cool. Let's give the guys Tuesday afternoon off.

Matthew had rubbed his temples. This was why you weren't supposed to start a relationship with a client, because he was required to say, *As per our contract, you'd still have to pay them for the time.*

She'd sent an eyes-crossed-tongue-sticking-out emoji, which he supposed meant she already knew that. Matthew didn't really speak emoji. He'd had to google some of the ones Jess had sent him, after googling how to use the emojis on his keyboard.

He'd been learning so much with her.

Like how, when he told her what he was feeling or thinking, she would respond in kind, sincerely—most of the time. She couldn't deny her nature completely, so some sarcasm was expected, but even still, everything had been so much easier than he'd anticipated so far. There hadn't even been any more crying.

There hadn't been any more sex either, but that was something Matthew was hoping to remedy that evening. He'd throw her over his shoulder and carry her out of the library if he had to.

Only it never came to that. Just as Matthew was making his final rounds through the inn, making sure all the lights were off before he left for the night, Jess and Nell tramped through the front door.

A jolt of electricity bolted Matthew's boots to the floor when he saw her for the first time in days. She had pulled her hair back, emphasizing the sharpness of her features. Her brow softened and her cheeks rounded as her lips curved into a smile when she saw him.

"Oh good," Nell said, reminding Matthew that she was there. "You're still here. You can help me convince Jess she's been spending too much time with Naomi, and the spook has taken hold of her."

Nell looked impeccable as usual, perfectly wavy hair and understated makeup, even at the end of the workday. And she was carrying—"Is that a picnic basket?"

"Nell wanted to come ghost hunting since she doesn't believe me," Jess said, as she walked right up to Matthew, popped up on the toes of her pointy boots, and kissed him on his nose. "So I told her she had to provide sustenance." Jess stepped back and patted the side of her messenger bag. "And I brought research while we wait for the ghosties."

Matthew felt his brow fold into a frown, even as his arms reached to pull Jess back into his embrace. "You two were going to do this by yourselves?"

Jess gave him a squeeze. "And you're going to protect us from the footsteps?" Her amusement was clear, but Matthew remembered the fear in her eyes the last few times they'd heard those very same footsteps.

"If it can shut doors, it can throw a saw at your head," he said.

Nell snorted. "Don't tell me you believe all this too."

Matthew shot her an annoyed look. "I have no idea what's happening here, but I know what I've seen. What I've heard, and something isn't right."

Nell made a prissy sort of harrumphing sound and shifted the picnic basket from one hand to the other. "Well, I refuse to spend any money on a psychic when I think it's hooey."

A raised eyebrow was Jess's only reaction to her partner's declaration. "You should stay," Jess said. "Unless you need to get some words down?"

Finally, an excuse to spend the evening with Jess. "Writing can wait," he was on the fence about telling her how much he'd missed her in front of Nell, but his expression must have communicated it, because Jess pulled her lower lip between her teeth in a way that had him wanting to tell Nell to buzz off. They could have their ghost hunt another night.

Instead, Nell said, "Okay, you two are cute, but if you start making out in front of me, I'm gone."

Jess winked at Matthew, like she was thinking the same thing he was. "We'll behave, cuz. Come on, if you have what I think you have in that picnic basket, I want to gorge myself."

Nell's picnic basket not only housed a huge array of vegetables, pita, hummus, and cheese, but a matching set of plates, silverware, and little metal cups she filled with sparkling water. They ate at the new breakfast table Nell had recently installed in the mostly finished attic. There were a few finishing touches to put on the space from Matthew's perspective. The rest was just decorating.

It had turned into a cozy apartment with the bed in the nook beneath the bank of windows, a sitting area nestled around a fireplace and a small kitchen in the far corner where they sat now, trying not to get hummus on the reams of paper Jess had brought along with her.

"What is all this?" Nell asked as she flipped through sheet after sheet of old records.

"I took a librarian up on her offer to make a deep dive into anything and everything she could find to do with this property since it was built. I figure she's the professional, and I've just been poking around." Jess patted the file folder in front of her. "This is just the first fifty years. She'll keep going if we don't find anything."

Matthew loved how excited she sounded, he just wished it was about something other than what he was sure would be a fruitless ghost search. Or it was possible he was jealous that this was what she'd been choosing over him for the last week.

After an hour of sifting through legal documents, Matthew had devolved into fantasizing about what he could be doing with Jess instead of this. The only noise in the attic was the sound of shuffling papers and the intermittent white noise from the furnace. A little kernel of satisfaction glowed in Matthew every time he heard it kick on. Installing the new furnace and making sure all the ductwork was up to code had been a son of a bitch, but the house was blessedly warm now. He didn't miss the space heaters in the slightest.

In fact, it was warm enough in the house now that if Matthew were to press Jess back into the new comforter on the bed in the corner and slowly peel every layer from her body, she might not even complain about the cold.

He was deep into imagining the texture of her skin beneath his hands when Nell said, "Hey, Matthew. Is your family from the area originally?"

The fantasy had become so real, it took him a moment to pull himself out of it, and when he did, it was with an inelegant "Huh?"

"Your family? Where are they from?"

He shrugged. "The farm out west had been in the family for generations. Why?"

Nell set a scanned newspaper article in the middle of the table. "Because I found this news article about a Wolfgang Zimmerman going missing during a cattle drive in 1907."

Matthew knew just enough about his family's history to understand that his dad's family was of German and Dutch ancestry, and his mother's family was French and Swiss. Whether there had ever been a Wolfgang in his family line, he wasn't sure. He wished his parents were still living. His dad would have known for sure. But perhaps there was something in the box of his father's things in the basement that could answer the question.

As Matthew read the article, he had to admit that it was possible. He knew his German ancestors had immigrated to the United States around the turn of the 20th century. And the missing man's home had been in the same county Matthew's family lived in now.

"It's possible there's a connection," he said. "But I don't think Wolfgang has anything to do with what's going on here."

A *thunk* sounded from across the room, and all three of them jumped.

"What the hell?" Matthew asked as he spotted his hammer on the floor by the bed. He'd been looking for the damn thing all day—again. None of the guys had seen it. He'd figured it must be in one of the other guy's toolboxes and he'd find it in the morning. He had no clue how it had gotten up here.

"Was that here the whole time?" Nell asked.

Jess was already crossing the room. She cocked her head to the side, examining where the hammer lay on the floor at the foot of the bed. She picked it up with two fingers near the base, held it to waist height, and dropped it. The sound it made when it landed on the wood floor was the same one they'd heard just a minute before.

Jess's wide eyes met Matthew's as he approached her. "How did that happen?" she asked him.

"I don't know," he said, swiping his hammer off the floor. It looked just like it normally did, was just as corporeal as it had always been. He had no clue how it could have possibly travelled from the first floor to the attic on its own.

"Maybe it's a sign?" Jess asked, though she sounded like she knew she was grasping.

"Like maybe it was Wolfgang?" Nell asked, skepticism clinging to her tone like a thick syrup.

Jess stepped up into Matthew, and he closed his arms around her, savoring the press of her body against his. The tightness in her muscles relaxed into him, and Matthew indulged himself with a kiss to the top of her forehead. "Do you think you could find out if there's any relation?" she asked him. "Between you and Wolfgang?"

Matthew traced up and down her spine beneath her ponytail for a moment, fighting his own skepticism. "I can do a little digging," he said. "Maybe my aunt will know something. She's the one who took over the farm when my gramps died." He didn't think it would have anything to do with this house. How could it? But if Jess was asking, he would give it to her without question.

"Naomi said that she thinks whoever is trapped here is trying to get our attention. I don't think anything is insignificant."

Matthew heard Nell say something about how Naomi was needlessly dramatic, but he ignored her, focusing on the woman in his arms instead. There was genuine concern in her eyes, as if she couldn't stand the idea of someone else's suffering.

And he understood then. She hadn't been digging through ancient newspapers as a lark. She'd been trying to help someone she didn't even know, and from the way she trembled, scared the daylights out of her.

"You are amazing," Matthew said, overcome with gratitude that he was allowed to hold this woman. Touch her. Kiss her.

Normally, he would have hesitated to give Jess more than a short, affectionate kiss in front of an audience, but right now he didn't give a damn what Nell thought. Matthew needed to worship Jess right now. He cupped her cheek, grazed his thumb over her bottom lip until her eyes met his and changed from distraught and frightened to captivated.

Then he brushed his lips over hers. Slowly. Gently. Barely a caress before pulling away to catch her eyes again. Captivation had given way to delight and a hint of impatience. So Matthew gave her what she wanted. A thorough, all-consuming kiss that used his tongue and his teeth. The nips at her lips meant to invoke their night together, to remind her of the heat and pleasure they'd shared the week before. To drive her need for more.

Jess's hand had just snaked up into the overlong hair at the base of Matthew's neck when he heard the first creak of a boot at the foot of the stairs. Jess stiffened in his arms. The door to the stairwell was directly across from them and closed. Since the night it had slammed, Matthew had closed it every time he'd had to work in the attic, and over the weeks, it had become a habit.

Matthew held his breath as the footsteps stopped just on the other side of the door, waiting for whatever might come next.

"Who is it?" Nell asked, like she was a kid not sure if she should answer a knock on the door.

Jess shushed her, but Nell looked at them like they were idiots as she passed them and moved to open the door. "It's probably one of the guys looking for Matthew."

As Nell neared the door, three knocks so hard that the door rattled in its frame sounded against the wood. Jess pulled Matthew closer, and Nell jumped back away from the door, her hand still stretched out toward the knob.

"Don't open it," Jess said.

But Nell didn't listen. Slowly, her fingers closed around the new brass knob and twisted. The door opened silently on its newly oiled hinges. Matthew had known there wouldn't be anyone there, but Nell mumbled something about it being too dark and was reaching for the stairwell light when there was a rushing, airy scream followed by the second set of light footsteps. The scream swept through the room as if carried on the wind, a cold breeze following behind it as the door slammed shut once again.

Nell backed away from the spot, shaking her head as if to deny what just happened. When she turned to face them, her face was white and she rubbed her arms as if she were chilled. "What the fuck just happened?" she asked, her voice as hoarse as if she'd just been the one screaming.

"That's what I've been trying to tell you," Jess said, stepping out of Matthew's arms and taking Nell's hands in her own. Jess led her to the bed and pulled her down to sit beside her. "Something strange is going on here, and we have to take care of it before we open and one of our guests dies of a heart attack or has a hammer fall on their head or something."

"This is so nuts," Nell said, shaking her head no over and over again. "How is it even real?"

Matthew was still coming to terms with it himself, and he and Jess had witnessed the events several times now. The sequence never changed much, but it seemed to be getting more violent, more urgent as time went on.

"I don't know," Jess said. "I don't understand it all, but if Naomi's friend can help, we need to bring him in."

Nell nodded.

Matthew shifted to pick up his hammer, and the floorboard creaked. Nell let out a yelp of surprise.

"Sorry," he said, holding his hands up to show the hammer. "I just wanted to put this away before it disappears again."

Jess shot him a knowing grin, but Nell still looked unsteady and pale. "I think I need to get out of here," she said.

"Sure," Jess said and pulled her to her feet. "We'll walk you out."

But it ended up being Matthew who walked Nell to her car. Jess, despite Matthew's objections, had stayed behind to clean.

From the street, the light from the attic shown like a beacon through the large bank of windows. Matthew wished he could see Jess. Leaving her by herself in that room for even a second just after all that activity made him anxious.

By the time he'd seen Nell off and made his way back upstairs, the food and dishes had been cleaned up, but the papers were still spread out on the table and Jess lay sprawled backward across the bed, her loose hair fanning out behind her.

"It's just me," he said as he crested the last stair.

She propped herself up on her elbows a teasing smile playing on her lips. "I know. You sound way different than

Randy." Then she patted the bed next to her, and Matthew understood why she'd been so insistent she stay behind.

As Matthew joined her on the bed, he forgot about everything that wasn't the silkiness of Jess's skin against his.

Chapter Twenty

1908
Mary

IT HAD BEEN TWO WEEKS since Mary had sent her letter to Josephina, the minister's wife who had helped her with her miscarriage, and the reply had finally arrived today. With only two days before the wedding, Mary had become so anxious, she'd taken to pacing the house, wringing her hands as she failed to think of a sustainable alternative if Josephina couldn't accomplish what Mary asked.

Mary had escaped to the attic with her letter the moment she'd returned from work and seen the envelope on the table in the front hall. The news had been better than Mary expected. The people trying to buy her parents' land were the family that owned the farm whose land joined the far side her parents' property. It was on the opposite side from where the ranch joined, but Mary knew the Kellys. Had known them her entire life, and they had been happy to work with her directly through a local lawyer to finalize the sale instead of through Frank.

They had nearly backed out multiple times because he'd been difficult to work with.

Apparently, he had been disrespectful on multiple occasions, implying that immigrant families didn't deserve to own land. Part of the reason the sale hadn't closed was that Frank had flat out told them that he was waiting for an offer from an American family who could pay a higher price, but that offer had fallen through, so the Kelly's had finally been accepted.

When it came to the inquiry into buying the ranch, Josephina admitted that it had been her family who had written to Mr. Black about the possibility. But it had only been an inquiry, and if Mary wanted to keep the property, they would be more than happy to help her move back in.

Mary held the letter to her heart, relief and gratitude flooding her in waves strong enough to soothe the anxiety she'd been carrying with her since Frank had decided they should get married. For the first time since Wolf had gone missing, Mary saw a way forward. There was a path that lay outside her circumstance, a course she wanted to take instead of the one her parents, her uncle, even Wolf had chosen for her.

Mary penned a reply as quickly as she was able, instructing Josephina to tell the Kellys that the land was as good as theirs, and that they would formalize the agreement as soon as Mary was back. And to cease any correspondence with Mr. Black, as his business practices weren't in alignment with her values. *Immigrant families shouldn't own land.* Her own family had barely been in the country fifty years. And where did Frank think her land had come from? Wolfgang had moved to Kansas *for* the promise of land.

Mary dashed to the post office to drop the letter in the mail before they closed for the day, her heart pounding in equal parts urgency and relief. She had told Josephina to expect her in a week. She was half tempted to set out today, but the journey would take planning, and she knew that if she ran, Frank would only chase her. She needed him to understand that there would be no following her.

She just hoped Lettie would be able to follow through on her part of the plan.

Chapter Twenty-One

2017
Jess

IT WOULD BE A LIE IF Jess said that one of the reasons she'd been hiding at the library in the evenings wasn't because she was afraid to sleep with Matthew again. Because she was terrified.

Did she want him? Unequivocally yes. More than that, she missed just hanging out with him. But she'd been more afraid of having another breakdown afterward than anything else. And needing to research the house so she could figure out how to get the damn thing unhaunted had been a convenient excuse to put just enough distance between them so that Matthew didn't think she was avoiding him, while also guaranteeing they were nowhere near a bed.

It was something a twenty-two year old might be able to get away with, but as a thirty-two year old, it was more than a little bit sad. The mature thing to do would be to tell him she was feeling gun-shy, but she'd been afraid he would take that the wrong way. Part of her knew better, that his behavior so far proved that he would give her all the time and space she wanted, but apparently, Jess even needed time to adjust to that.

But when she'd seen Matthew tonight? When they'd started making out before the ghosts had shown up and spoiled everything, Jess had known she'd been behaving like a monumental idiot by trying to avoid him.

This man made her feel alive. Fearless. Brave.

And that was saying something considering everything that had been going on.

Jess stretched out, her skin relishing the luxurious feel of the new sheets in the bed she and Matthew had just christened. Maybe it was a little crazy after what had just happened, but for Jess, the incident that had scared Nell out of the inn hadn't been nearly as important as getting naked with Matthew after that kiss. He'd come back upstairs after seeing Nell out, and they hadn't said a word. They hadn't needed to. Matthew had kissed every part of her body, and she'd taken him in her mouth, licking and sucking until he'd cursed and pulled her up his body.

And when she'd sunk down on top of him. The fullness, the stretch and ache of her body had completed her in a way she hadn't expected. But instead of fearing what finding pleasure like this meant, she'd embraced the ecstasy instead.

And she hadn't shed a tear afterward.

Jess had come so hard, she'd laughed. She'd *never* laughed before. She was pretty sure she'd been smiling when she fell asleep.

Granted, now that she was awake, she had zero clue what time it was, but Matthew was still asleep in the bed beside her, and that was all that mattered. She snuggled further into his side, her fingers finding the smattering of chest hair on his sternum and skimming back and forth over the coarse yet soft hair. Jess never thought she'd be into chest hair, but she was finding that there was no part of Matthew she didn't enjoy.

It only occurred to her that her explorations had the possibility of waking him when his arm tightened around her waist and his leg shifted against hers.

Her hand left his chest abruptly, and with a sleepy sort of chuckle, Matthew said, "That felt good. Why'd you stop?" His voice was deep and gravelly with sleep. Jess wanted to capture it inside her and pull it out on her high-anxiety days to use as a balm for her psyche.

"I didn't mean to wake you."

He rolled to face her, pulling her against his front so that they touched from their foreheads to where her toes brushed against his shins. "I do not mind. Why are you awake?"

Jess kissed his nose instead of answering. She didn't know why she was awake. Her body was alert and aware, and she had no reason to be. Her prevailing theory was that her body was just excited to be so close to his.

Matthew captured her lips with his when she didn't answer, and she moaned into it. It was most definitely her desire for him that had awakened her. To Jess's delight, Matthew didn't need much coaxing. He rolled her underneath him all while palming her breasts and running his hard length over her folds.

Despite avoiding him, Jess had tucked a string of condoms into her purse, just to make doubly sure they were protected until she could get on birth control. The string was still on the bedside table, and Matthew made quick work of sheathing himself before teasing his way slowly, oh-so slowly, inside her.

"Fuck, Jess." His voice was still that gravely rasp in her ear, and she clenched around him involuntarily. A free-floating part of her mind thought that if she ever heard him sing one of his bluegrass songs, she might orgasm on the spot.

"I know," she gasped between kisses. "You feel so good."

Matthew swore again and maneuvered one thumb so it was sandwiched between them, hitting that spot he'd discovered their first night together.

"Shit, Matthew. Yes."

His response was a satisfied growl and harder, deeper thrusts that had Jess losing her breath altogether. She wanted to tell him he was perfect, that together, they were more than she'd ever hoped for, but she didn't have the brainpower to form words as Matthew drove into her, lost to his own bliss.

The pressure of his thumb, the weight of his body, the reach of his cock, the urgent caress of his lips against hers all sent Jess spiraling so much sooner than she'd expected. She embraced the euphoria, even as she didn't want it to be over yet. Until Matthew cursed again, and she knew he was going over the edge with her. Knowing they were alone in this giant house, Jess allowed herself to scream her release until the laughter overtook her again. This time, Matthew joined her, chuckling deeply as he laid kisses over her neck and shoulders.

"Holy shit, Jess. I fucking love you so much." His lips captured hers, and he mimicked the motion he'd just been doing with his hips with his mouth before pulling away from her.

Jess couldn't see much more than his outline, but she knew he was getting rid of the condom. She stretched, settling back into the perfect cushion of the mattress, knowing she should get up and make use of the new bathroom, but not ready to leave the warmth of the bed yet.

Matthew had just ducked back under the covers with her when the footsteps came. They were louder and more menacing in the middle of the night, with darkness pressing around them from all sides. Jess had forgotten they even existed, but as she hid her face in Matthew's chest, she chastised herself for not expecting them.

He squeezed her body into his, turning his back to the door as if he could protect her from the sound. The door was closed, and just like earlier, once the footsteps reached the top of the stairs, a pounding knock rattled the door against the frame.

Jess couldn't help it, she tucked herself more deeply into Matthew's embrace as the doorknob shook, like the ghost was trying to get in. Jess felt like he was trying to get to *them*. Somehow, she knew that if he got into the room, he would try to do them harm. She had no idea what he thought he could do or where the conviction came from, but she knew that if he was able to open that door, something bad would happen.

That was when a breeze picked up inside the room. Jess felt the whoosh of cool air breeze past the bed as the woman's footsteps flew towards the door, slamming against the energy there with a scream so fierce Jess had to cover her ears.

And just as quickly as it had started, it was all over. The feeling of dread, the cold temperature, the certainty of danger. All of it was gone. The attic apartment was serene and quiet once again.

"Is this escalating?" Jess asked, "Because I feel like it's escalating."

She felt Matthew's nod, then his lips, as he placed a kiss on the top of her head. "We should get out of here before it comes back."

Jess clung to Matthew, not ready to leave the perceived safety of his arms, the protection of the comforter. Not ready to descend the dark stairs and venture out into the cold, dark night. Definitely not ready to go home alone.

"Will you come home with me?" she asked.

"Of course." His hands skimmed up and down her back like he didn't want to let her go yet either, but with a quick pat to her backside he sat up and threw back the covers. The room was still chilled on the other side of the blankets, and Jess scrambled for her clothes and locked herself in the bathroom to get dressed, like that would somehow protect her.

When she emerged, Matthew had made the bed and organized the research she'd brought into a neat pile on the table. She rushed to shove the pile into her messenger bag. Matthew entwined his fingers through hers, and she practically cut off his circulation when he turned off the lights and they left the house using the flashlight on his phone.

The street was silent, but tranquil. Jess could immediately feel the difference from the humming of potential chaos inside the house. She'd never noticed it before, but even when the activity was quiet, there was an energy buzzing in the background, like a current of electricity. But outside it was just quiet. Cold. She looked up and could make out a few stars through the streetlights. She took comfort in the cloudless night sky.

"Come back for your car in the morning?" Matthew asked.

"Sounds like a plan to me."

As they pulled away from the curb, Jess studied the house through the window, and she could have sworn she saw something move in the attic.

Chapter Twenty-Two

Matthew

JESS'S ALARM SOUNDED about five seconds after Matthew shut his eyes. It had been after three when they'd left the inn for Jess's apartment, and almost four by the time they'd climbed into bed. The heavy satisfaction of good sex coupled with good old-fashioned exhaustion helped to pull him into slumber quickly, despite the heavy processing that was happening in the back of his mind. He'd been dreaming of footsteps and hadn't understood where he was until Jess groaned and flipped her alarm off.

She rolled over and pressed herself into Matthew's side, which helped remind him of the more pleasant aspects of the previous evening. Being with her like this, waking up with her, making love to her. Hell, having her let her guard down enough just to let him touch her was basically a miracle. Now if only they could have all of that without an angry, jealous ghost coming after them.

Matthew had almost given in to the pull of sleep again when his alarm went off this time.

He puffed out a breath. He didn't even know where his phone was. That it wasn't dead on the floor of the attic was a wonder in and of itself.

He found it plugged in on the table next to his side of the bed. Had he done that? Had Jess? He couldn't remember much more than opening the new toothbrush Jess had handed him and collapsing into bed. It would have been really great if it was a weekend, but it was Friday. They both had to get out of bed and go to work. Which was exactly the last thing Matthew wanted to do.

Jess squirmed against him as he collapsed back against the pillow and sighed. The peaked tips of her breasts pressed into his side, and Matthew wanted to spend the morning worshipping them instead. He'd never explored her in the daylight before. Tracing her body with his lips without the veil of shadow and moonlight was the only option as far as his body was concerned.

Jess wiggled right into his morning wood and then did it again on purpose.

Matthew cupped one round, firm cheek and pressed her hips against his until she hissed. "It's not nice to tease," he said.

"Who said I was teasing?"

"Do we have time?" he asked.

Jess rolled on top of him, a condom already squeezed between her fingers. "Does it matter?"

"Where did that come from?"

"I grabbed it when I turned off my phone. I thought it might come in handy."

And it did.

He'd driven her back to the inn after they'd both showered, but he met her back at her place for dinner when he was done at work, and they didn't leave the apartment for the rest of the weekend. By Sunday night, Matthew was fairly certain he shouldn't have been able to walk, but instead he felt invigorated, like after a good session at the gym, only better.

They'd spent the few hours they weren't in bed sifting through the rest of Jess's research. They found out that the original owner of the house had owned what was basically a drug store with a sandwich counter, and that his wife had died before they'd been able to have children. The house had been sold a handful of times after that. There were still a few piles left to go through, but so far, the most promising lead had been the missing cowboy who shared Matthew's last name.

That was why, on Sunday evening, they were headed back to his house. Well, Matthew also needed fresh clothes, but he had told Jess about the box of his father's things, and she'd insisted they go through that before tackling the rest of the papers.

He thought she was after some excitement since most of the files they'd been through had been local news about the homeowners. Weddings, births, anniversaries, deaths—none of which had happened in the home or seemed at all suspicions. There had been no reports of domestic violence or any incident that even remotely sounded like it would have anything to do with the ominous footsteps. Unless one of the residents of the attic apartment had been particularly fond of clomping around just to frighten the other tenants of the house to death.

Jess had opened a bottle of wine and unpacked the sandwiches they'd purchased on the way over. It turned out Jess didn't cook either. If they were going to be in this relationship for real, one of them was going to have to figure out how to use a stove. They couldn't live off of takeout forever.

The box was covered in years' worth of dust, and the contents inside weren't much better, but Matthew pulled out the file of genealogical research his father had started doing after his diagnosis. The cancer treatments had made it impossible for him to teach at the local high school any longer, but on his good days, his dad had gone to the local historical society and put together what he could about the people who'd first purchased the Zimmerman Ranch property.

His aunt had the old family Bible, and he'd sent her a text to ask if they'd ever had an ancestor called Wolfgang, but she was so busy, even in the winter, he didn't expect her to text him back for a few days.

He recounted the few memories he had of his family from when he was younger. He'd met his great-great-grandmother once, when he was about five years old. She was living in an assisted living facility with a friend of hers. The occasion had been her 100th birthday, but she'd passed not long after. And he didn't remember her name. Everyone had called her Mama or Mama Zimmerman like she was everyone's mother. Which, he supposed, in a way, she had been.

Then there was the story that his great-great-grandfather had been the one to move to Kansas from Germany, but Matthew didn't remember any extraordinary stories about him. He'd have thought that if there were anything as sensational as the man disappearing, it would have become one of the family stories told over and over again. They still lived on the same property for goodness sake.

But Matthew was coming up frustratingly empty on anything other than his grandfather's stories of squaring off with a bull who had jumped a fence or of herding errant cattle off the highway and back onto the pasture they'd broken out of. Any stories that predated the Korean War had been lost to Matthew.

Jess basically inhaled her sandwich, ignored her pretzels, and had barely touched her wine, all in anticipation of getting her hands on the file. He understood her motivation for wanting to do what she could to get rid of the ghosts and protect her investments, but she was having a lot more fun with this research process than he was.

Matthew was the author, the one with a journalism degree, he should be a lot more interested in what they were doing than he was. Sure, some of it was fascinating, but Matthew was fighting off foreboding so thick, he could hardly chew his roast beef sandwich, let alone swallow it down without a thick sip of wine.

His fear made no sense. There was nothing in his family history, but it was as if the atmosphere in the room had changed when Jess had started leafing through the file folder full of yellowing sheaths of paper. It felt the way the attic did when the heavy footsteps started up the stairs. But the only sound Matthew heard was the instrumental music he'd switched on and the swish of shuffling paper.

Was it possible something had followed them home from the job site? The whole weekend had been quiet at Jess's house. He stood, pacing out the length of the room, looking for something out of place while Jess leafed through his father's notes and article clippings. He had never taken the time to go through any of it, so he had no idea what she was finding out about his family's past.

Matthew found himself standing at the bookshelf, sipping his nearly empty glass of the red wine that was Jess's favorite. He thought it tasted like someone had spread decades old jelly on pressboard and tossed it in a blender. That he was drinking it without complaining was proof of how much he loved her. And he would do it in the future too, but he'd also told her that he preferred his favorite brand of beer, without telling her he thought wine was disgusting, and he saw her put the two together.

He liked how easy it was to be honest with her without being harsh or having to get into a fight about it. He'd never felt comfortable being open this early in a relationship. He had always still been stuck on trying to impress the woman he was seeing. Matthew's relationships never lasted much past that stage.

What he was building with Jess was different. He didn't need a long courtship to know that this was the woman he was going to be with for the rest of his life.

Matthew was just thinking that he should ask Jess how she felt about marriage when a book fell off its shelf in the far corner of the room. Jess barely seemed to notice; she was scrutinizing a copy of a photograph on printer paper.

The hair on the back of Matthew's neck stood up as he approached. None of the books on his shelves were perched near the edge. The line of dust visible in the spot where this book had been clearly marked that there had been a good inch between the book and the edge. Matthew had so many books, they were crammed into the shelves. None of them were loose or falling over. The chances that this book could have fallen on its own were slim.

"What are you doing here?" he said, as he knelt to pick up the volume. He wasn't sure if he was asking the book or the protective ghost he thought of as a woman. The one who kept slamming the door to prevent the ghost on the stairs from getting into the attic.

He had absolutely no reason to think that she was the reason the book had landed on the floor, but it was as good an explanation as any.

The book was his grandfather's journal, which Matthew had forgotten even existed, let alone that it was in his possession. He would have always assumed his aunt would have kept it. She had always been their grandfather's favorite.

"Has the banjo always been, like, a thing in your family?" Jess asked from across the room.

Matthew looked down at the journal in his hands, then back over at Jess, who had spread copies of photographs over his coffee table.

"My grandfather taught me. We spent summers out on the family farm, and he played. Every evening on the porch. He said his grandfather had taught him the same way."

"Is this your grandfather, do you think?" she showed him a photograph that looked like it had been taken in the fifties. And old man with a wrinkled face and a young boy sat on a set of porch steps, each with a banjo in their laps. The boy's banjo looked comically large compared to his small size, but they were both smiling at the camera.

"That looks like the farmhouse," he said and flipped the paper over like it might have their names scrawled on the back.

"Have you found his name yet?" Matthew asked, tapping the photo of the older gentleman.

"Just a couple references to Papa Zim in notes. No proper name or actual records or anything. What's that?"

Matthew handed over the book. "It was my grandfather's journal."

"Have you ever read it?" she asked.

"I've flipped through it a time or two, but his handwriting was atrocious."

Jess snorted as she leafed through the pages. "What we need is a family tree or a timeline or something," she said.

"Do you really think this is related to what's going on at the inn?"

Jess reached for her glass of wine and leaned back on the sofa as she scanned his grandfather's scrawl. "I don't know. I mean I don't know where else to look. This is all just so improbable." She took a long sip of her wine and said, "I'm honestly just looking for whatever distraction I can think of until Craig comes on Tuesday and tells us what to do about it all."

"Craig?"

"Naomi's actually psychic friend. I guess he's a medium or something."

"The psychic's name is Craig?"

"What's wrong with that?" Jess asked, even as she bit her bottom lip to keep from smiling in answer to the grin plastered over his lips.

"I don't know, I just would expect a psychic to have a more mystical sounding name, like Astral Projection or Zenith or something ridiculous."

"Astral Projection as a name?"

He shrugged. "Well, it's a stage name, obviously."

"Obviously," Jess said and focused her attention back on the book. Matthew flipped through the photographs Jess had laid out. All taken at the farm, all older relatives he'd either never met or couldn't recognize looking so young. Matthew knew he'd been born to teenage parents; it was one of the reasons the farm had gone to his aunt, because Matthew's father had always been preoccupied with whatever kept him close to Matthew's mother. That was the main thing he remembered about the two of them, their devotion to each other. Working their way through school together, working at the same school when they'd finally graduated, dying of cancer only months apart. His mother's cervical, his father's prostate. But seeing the photos of them so young, so healthy, and so alive was like a kick to the gut and a soft summer breeze all at once.

One photograph was dated 1962 and pictured his grandfather holding and tossing Matthew's toddler-aged father high. Doing the math, his grandfather would have been only eighteen in 1962, and his dad had to have been at least a year old in that photo. He looked for more, older photographs, curious to see proof of the old family tradition of falling in love hard and having kids young. Everyone but Matthew and his aunt.

That was probably another thing Matthew and Jess should discuss. He had no idea how she felt about kids. She'd been spectacular with Jackson, but did that mean she wanted children of her own? He didn't know. He'd always assumed he would have kids. Hell, Matthew was already the same age his grandfather had been when he'd been born. Matthew barely felt old enough to be an adult, let alone a *grandparent.*

"Your Mama Zim sounds like an interesting woman," she said as she turned the page in his grandfather's journal.

"How are you even reading that?" he asked.

She shrugged. "It's like a code. Once I figured out a few words, it was easier to decipher the rest. Anyway, did you know your Mama Zim was basically a witch?"

Matthew snorted. "What? Like Naomi?"

Jess tapped his knee with the tip of her gray suede booties. They were the same pair she'd been wearing the day she'd given him the keys to the house. "Not like Naomi, like in the way that used to get women burned at the stake."

"So what, she grew herbs in the woods?" Matthew, who had been searching through the box of papers for other photographs, found a stack of actual photos that had been tucked into a file. Some were so old, he was afraid to touch them.

"More like she was a midwife, and locals came to her for herbal remedies and stuff. Your grandfather talks about how there were always women and babies hanging around the house when he was a kid, and they were always working with plants while the men were out working with the cattle."

Matthew unearthed a photograph of the woman in question then. An original print he didn't dare lift to show Jess. One corner had already crumbled away. He didn't know how he knew it was her, but it had to be. She was a young blonde woman wearing a soft-looking light colored dress. He guessed it was from the early 20th century.

"I think this is her," Matthew said, and Jess leaned forward to peer at the photo.

"I bet you're right." She cocked her head to the side. "Your sister looks just like her, only with darker hair."

Matthew could see what she meant. The oval shape of her face, the structure of brow and nose did remind him of Dana.

Jess slipped a loose sheet of paper under the photo, then carefully covered it with another and gently turned it over. On back, in fading ink, it read, "Mary, on her marriage to Wolfgang. 1903."

The writing was clear and legible. It definitely read Wolfgang.

"Do you think that's the same Wolfgang who disappeared?" Jess asked.

Matthew frowned. "If he did, then who's this?" Matthew tapped the image of his two forebears playing the banjo on the porch together.

"Maybe she married his brother?" Jess said.

"Maybe," Matthew said, still not sure how any of this had anything at all to do with the activity at the house and anxious they weren't getting anywhere.

Chapter Twenty-Three

Jess

THE HOUSE LOOKED BIGGER on Tuesday. As if it had grown since she and Matthew had sneaked out of it in the wee hours of Friday morning. Jess hadn't been back since then, but Matthew had gone back to work Monday morning like it was no big deal. Jess hadn't been able to shake the pure terror she'd felt as whatever was on the other side of the door had tried to get into the room. She'd had no doubt that whoever he was, he was after them.

She did not want to go back inside. Even as she knew Matthew was waiting for her in the attic. His was the only truck left on the street. The other guys had all left already. She stayed on the sidewalk out front, waiting for Naomi and Craig to arrive. Was she selfish, leaving him in there by himself?

Who was she kidding? He probably wasn't in the attic. More than likely he was in the kitchen double-checking that all the appliances that had arrived that morning were installed correctly. She'd noticed that about him. He trusted his men to do their work, but he signed off on everything before he let Jess and Nell know that it was finished. He was a little bit of a perfectionist, her Matthew.

Her Matthew.

The idea made Jess's insides go gooey.

Her Matthew.

Was it too soon to think of him that way? They hadn't had any discussions about who they were to each other, but she knew Matthew would be insulted if she asked him what kind of relationship he thought they had. He had long-term written on his soul. And spending the last two days buried in his grandfather's journal had made her love him and his family. His parent's might be gone, but Matthew had a history. A place to go back to, and even if none of it was related to what was happening in the house, Jess was glad they had discovered it all together.

A car pulled up behind Jess, but she didn't look. She was too busy steeling herself for whatever might happen once they went inside. She had no idea what to expect, but she couldn't shake the feeling the ghosts weren't going to like Jess's attempts to move them out.

"What the hell happened to your hair?" came a voice from behind Jess. And not the voice she'd expected.

Jess turned on her heel. Instead of her sister, it was the last person Jess wanted to see, or at least, the last person she wanted commenting on her disastrous visit to the salon that morning. Her normal stylist had called in sick, but Jess had been in such desperation for a trim, she said she'd take the new girl. Only the new girl apparently didn't know how to style curly hair, so she'd straightened it. Jess had tried to go with it, telling herself it was a new adventure, that she'd be fine. She could wash it in the morning, and it would be back to its usual voluminous glory, but that still meant she had to spend an antsy day with hair that didn't feel like hers. She wasn't going to explain any of that to Ana. It wasn't any of her business anymore.

"What the hell are you doing here?" Jess asked.

"I came to see the progress on the house," she said, like it was obvious. Like architects just dropped by whenever they wanted after their job was done.

"Did you have an appointment?" Jess asked. "Because we're not really in the position to give a tour this afternoon."

Ana gave her that same maddening smile she'd started using on Jess in the last couple of years of their relationship. The smile that said Jess was adorable and extremely stupid. It brought Jess straight back to that vulnerable, precipitous emotional state she'd spent most of the last year in, unsure of her place in the world, doubting not just her convictions, but her intelligence, her entire sense of self, and she hated it. Jess hadn't felt that way in months. She hadn't missed it.

Jess squared her shoulders and did her best to feel confident, but she knew she looked more defiant than anything. It didn't help that Ana was dressed impeccably. She wore a black pencil skirt and heeled boots under her black wool coat. Her hair was its winter shade of chestnut brown and had grown out of its pixie cut just enough to look adorably disheveled.

"I ran into Nell. She mentioned you were having a little bit of trouble with the supernatural, and I had to see for myself."

Jess rolled her eyes. Likely story. She wondered what else she'd heard from Nell. Jess thought it was more likely that Ana had been stalking Jess's social media and seen the selfies she'd made Matthew take with her over the weekend and called Nell to get the story.

They hadn't seen one another since October, hadn't really spoken since a month before that. But the second Jess started a new relationship, here Ana was, letting Jess know that none of her decisions were beyond judgement or reproach.

"Our business isn't here for your entertainment," Jess said.

She heard the front door open behind her and tossed a look over her shoulder to see Matthew striding down the porch steps, a concerned frown crumpling his brow. He hadn't shaved for days, and he basically had a full-blown beard going on. Maybe she could convince him to keep it. A beard looked sexy as hell on him, and Jess realized she'd broken into a smile as she'd watched him approach.

"Hey," he said, kissing Jess on the forehead. "You just get here?"

"Yup." She purposefully popped the *p* and nodded toward her ex-girlfriend. "And Ana has invited herself to our walk-through."

"Hey, Ana. How's it going?"

Matthew stepped forward and offered his hand, but Ana's disdainful gaze bounced from his hand to his face, to Jess, and back to his hand. Matthew dropped his hand with a shake of his head. "That's a little petty, don't you think?" he asked, and Jess wanted to kiss him for it.

Ana pursed her lips. "It's not very ethical to be in a relationship with one of your clients, either, but I don't see that stopping you," Ana said with a pitying smile.

"It's really none of your business," Jess said, but even to herself she sounded like a petulant teenager.

Matthew shot her a quiet grin, like he understood every changing emotion that was tearing through Jess at the moment.

"I like your hair," he said. "I've never seen it straight before." Then he ran his hands through where the ends reached to the dip of her waist. "It's so long like this."

"I tried a new stylist today, and it was a disaster."

He wrapped a lock around his finger, and let it unravel. "I think it's cute, but I understand if you prefer it curly."

"The giant hair makes her nose look smaller by comparison," Ana said, startling both Jess and Matthew, who had already forgotten she was there.

"Jesus, Ana. Stop being a bitch and just let Jess be happy."

Jess whipped around to see her sister and a tall, reedy man approaching from the other direction. Naomi wrapped an arm around Jess's shoulders and squeezed. "I've always got your back," she whispered in Jess's ear.

"Thanks," Jess picked at a fold of the purple velvet cloak Naomi wore. "I like your cloak."

"Isn't it amazing? Look." Naomi flipped back the fabric to reveal the gray faux-fur lining. "It has pockets, and it's, like, the warmest thing I've ever worn." Then she twirled in a circle that had the cloak billowing around her legs, pure delight on her face. "Anyway, Jess, Matthew, this is Craig."

Craig nodded at each of them, then turned his attention back to the house. Like his name, Craig just looked like a regular guy. His pants were a little too short, his coat a little baggy, and his glasses were a little crooked. He looked like he should be somebody's IT guy, not a professional psychic.

"Craig and I just took a walk around the block so he could get a feel for the neighborhood. I haven't told him anything except that you're experiencing activity that's steadily elevating. We're ready to get started as soon as Nell arrives."

Jess shook her head, "Nell's not coming. It's just the three of us."

"Excellent," Naomi beamed. "Craig are you ready?" The man nodded, even as he kept his gaze on the house.

Naomi turned to Ana. "It was an absolute nightmare seeing you again, Ana, but unfortunately, it's time for you to leave."

Ana didn't look like she was done being outraged about Naomi calling her a bitch, but she definitely didn't like being told what to do, and had opened her mouth to say something when Craig said, "She should stay." He started up the front walk and the rest of them followed him.

Ana shot a glare at Jess and Naomi over her shoulder as she stalked past them, taking up the spot directly behind Craig like she was the lead on this project. As per usual.

Jess glanced over her shoulder at Matthew, who raised his eyes from where he'd been checking out her ass with a sheepish smile. She returned it, thankful to feel the rush of heat and love and desire as he pushed up the sleeves of his old hoody, like he was hot in twenty-degree weather.

She was still annoyed that Ana was there, but it was a relief to find that even if Ana's attitude made Jess feel like shit in general, nothing about her feelings for Matthew wavered in the face of her former lover's disdain. Knowing that made Jess not mind so much about Ana's opinion in general. If Ana wanted to continue to be a mean, hateful shrew, that was up to her. It didn't have any bearing on Jess's life anymore, and she wouldn't allow it any room to gain purchase again.

Once inside, Craig just sort of wandered around the ground floor, asking questions occasionally about the age of the house and the work they'd been doing.

"I thought you were going with blue in the entry way instead of gray. Blue would have been more welcoming," Ana had said when they'd first come in.

Craig had cut that off with a "Please, no talking unless I ask you a direct question." Then with a tender smile to Naomi, he said, "Unless you have any clarifying questions."

Jess raised her eyebrows at her sister. She didn't think Craig was quite her sister's type, but with Naomi, it was never safe to assume. Naomi gave a minute shake of her head, the gleam in her eyes promising a story for a different day.

They spent the next twenty minutes trailing Craig through the house. Jess spent the time appreciating how well the project was coming together. The house truly was beautiful, and with the work Matthew and his crew had been doing, you never would have known it had been a decrepit shell of a house six months ago. As soon as it was warm enough, the outside would be painted and the landscaper would come in, and their sparkling new inn would look better than any other house on the street.

If they were able to get rid of the ghosts.

Craig stopped at the stairwell to the attic, gazing up into the darkness. "This is where you're experiencing the most activity?"

"Yes," Jess said. She'd been about to explain the footsteps, but then Craig was clomping up the stairs, mimicking the exact tone and rhythm of the steps they'd been hearing. Matthew entwined his fingers with hers and squeezed. Then they watched Craig stop at the top of the stairs.

"The footsteps you've been hearing belong to a man who used to rent the room, maybe one hundred years ago," he said, then went into the attic.

Jess and Matthew followed him first, Naomi and Ana trailing behind them.

Craig was running his hand over the duvet when they joined him. He looked Jess right in the eye and said, "You need to wash these sheets." Then he smiled and said, "Congratulations on the new relationship by the way," with a nod to their clasped hands.

Then he paced the room, and seemed to pick up a rhythm, pacing the same few feet over and over, even as he seemed to be listening to something.

Naomi seemed drawn to the bed also, while Ana hovered in the doorway.

"I'm hearing from a dead woman," Craig said. "She passed in her nineties, maybe later, but she's presenting to me as a girl in her early twenties. Blonde hair. She's wearing a wedding dress. She's been trapped here by the man in the stairs."

"Why did he trap her?" Naomi asked.

"He thinks she belongs to him."

Craig's eyes shot to where Ana stood in the stairwell door. "He says that if it weren't for the German, she would have been his in life. But now she is his forever. She's put a barrier on the doorway so he can't get in, but you two," he looked at Matthew and Jess, "your love agitates him. He doesn't want anyone in your family to find happiness."

"My family?" Matthew asked, touching his free hand to his chest.

"Your family is her family," Craig said. "The one she had in life. She keeps calling you her son, but I'm guessing she's a distant ancestor at best.

"Mary?" Jess asked. "His great-great-grandmother was Mary Zimmerman."

Craig nodded noncommittally. And nodded back to the stairwell. Ana had moved to the side, a look of smug disbelief on her face, but also placing herself out of the direct line of fire. "There are only the two people," he said, "but there's an imprint on the stairs that keeps playing over and over again. He's keeping me from seeing everything clearly, but there's a second man, the one he keeps calling The German. There's an altercation that ends with the death of the man who lives in the stairway."

"Were they fighting over Mary?" Naomi asked.

Craig nodded, watching the stairwell as if he were seeing it all unfold in front of him. "The other man, the German, was her husband, but I'm not sure about when they were married. The dead man was her lover. But she keeps calling the German your father," he said to Matthew.

Jess clung to Matthew, at once excited and terrified to learn that there was a connection to Matthew's family.

"Again, I think she's confused. She keeps telling me how much you look like your father." Craig grimaced like he was getting a little annoyed by it, but Jess supposed she could understand that.

"Is there anything we can do?" she asked.

Craig shrugged. "I have to get out of here. All of us being up here is stirring up trouble."

He and Naomi left, but Ana blocked Jess and Matthew from descending the stairs, standing with feet wide, arms crossed, and a superior smirk on her face. "You don't actually think that guy is for real, do you?" she asked, her eyes zeroing in on Jess.

"Everything he said seems consistent with what we've experienced." She had to concentrate not to shift from foot to foot under Ana's scrutiny. Not because it was Ana, but because she wanted to squeeze past her and get down the stairs and away from the attic. The air around them was turning cold, and Jess was getting goosebumps under her sweater.

"Oh, you've been hearing footsteps, so now there's a dead guy who hangs out in the stairwell?" Ana let out a laugh. "I hope you didn't pay him too much to fill your mind with nonsense."

"Ana, it doesn't matter, okay," Matthew said. He let go of Jess's hand for the first time since they entered the attic. "Let's just go downstairs."

Instead Ana stepped forward, poking Matthew in the chest, right on the zipper of his worn-out hoodie. "And you. Don't think I'll be recommending your company to anyone again." Then she turned her finger on Jess, but Matthew stepped back out of Ana's reach, pulling Jess with him.

"Was this why you hired him?" Ana asked as she advance into the room. "Was this going on from the beginning."

"No, I—"

But Ana cut her off. "The two of you make me sick."

"That's enough, Ana," Matthew said, his harsh voice, leaving no room for argument. "You and Jess had been over for months before she and I even shared something as personal as a cup of coffee."

Jess remembered that cup of coffee. It might have been the moment she'd started falling for him. Finding her courage, Jess stood up straighter. "Please, Ana. Show some dignity. It's over. It's been over for six months. Just let it be."

Ana's lip curled as if she were going to say something truly revolting when the footsteps started up the stairs. Ana flipped around and gasped, stumbling back when she saw no one in the stairwell, even as the sound of the boots drew nearer.

"What the fuck is that?" Ana said, terror making her voice rise.

"We call him Randy," Matthew said. He sounded casual, even as he pulled Jess closer, and angling her away from the door.

"This is so ridiculous," she said, shaking her head, "It can't be."

The footsteps stopped at the top of the stairs like usual. Silence hung in the air like thunderclouds. Jess held her breath and waited for lightning to strike. She waited for Mary's footsteps, the scream and whoosh of cold air that came with the effort it took for her to slam the door and shut Randy out. But it didn't come.

Jess looked from the doorway to Ana, to Matthew. He met her eyes, swallowed, and looked back toward the doorway. As he did another footstep sounded, the final step from the stairwell onto the landing in the attic. One step further than they'd ever come before. And then another.

And another.

Ana crumpled to the floor like someone had shoved her hard in the chest.

Matthew pushed Jess behind him, walking them backward across the room toward the bed. If he said anything, Jess couldn't hear him. All she heard were the sound of boots on wood echoing in the big, open space and the rush of her blood in her ears.

He was coming for Jess. She didn't know why or how he'd worked his way past Mary's barrier, but the attic had filled with nothing but the overwhelming sense of menace.

But what could she or Matthew or anyone do against something they couldn't see?

The backs of Jess's knees hit the edge of the mattress and she toppled backward onto the bed. Matthew covered her with his body offering what protection he could as the footsteps crept nearer, still the sound of boots against wood, even as they crossed the area rug in front of the bed.

They stopped, right next to the bed; an invisible hand depressed the mattress just to the right of Jess's head. She could hear a raspy breath next to her ear, so opposite from Matthew's quick, heavy breathing. Just as the weight on the bed shifted closer to them, the loudest scream Jess had ever heard rent through every other sound in the room. The temperature dropped, and with a great whoosh, the third body left the bed and the door slammed shut, leaving the room freezing and silent.

Slowly, like melting ice, sound crept back into the space. Jess heard Matthew heave in air like he'd been holding in his breath. Then she heard the furnace kick on.

There were footsteps on the stairs, not the slow steady tread of the ghost, but swift and light, more like Mary's.

But it wasn't one of the ghosts at all. Naomi screamed for Jess as she reached the top of the stairs. She pounded on the door, and turned the doorknob, but it was as if the door was barred.

It took all three of them a moment to register what was happening. Matthew clung to Jess as she pushed herself to sitting on the bed. Ana rubbed her chest as she rose to standing.

"Jess!" Naomi screamed as she pulled on the knob. "Jess, please be okay. I didn't mean to leave you. I thought you were right behind me." She pounded on the door again, and the sob at the tail end of her sister's words broke the spell of shock that Jess had been under.

"I'm here," she said. "We're all fine."

Jess heard Ana mutter "Speak for yourself" under her breath as she rubbed at her sternum some more, but Jess ignored her as she tried the door.

The knob didn't turn.

Jess turned the lock and tried again to no avail.

Panic rose up, and she pulled on the door before she remembered Craig's words about a barrier. Maybe Mary was still trying to protect them?

"Please, let us out. It's my sister. My family. And once we're out, I will do what I can to help you. I promise."

Mathew had crossed the room while Jess had bargained with the ghost. He kissed Jess on the forehead, placed his hand over hers on the knob, and the door clicked open.

Chapter Twenty-Four

1908
Mary

MARY WANTED TO SCREAM, but she couldn't find her voice. She scrambled backward across the bed until her back hit the windows, and still the figure approached, his footsteps echoing across the room in ominous clunks of his boots against the hardwood.

Oh, God. No. She'd yearned for some proof that Wolfgang was gone, but not like this. Not his spirit come for her on the day she was supposed to marry another man.

Tears poured down her cheeks, and she realized she was crying. Babbling nonsense about how she wasn't going to marry Frank through her tears.

And then he was kneeling on the bed, his filthy hands coming to rest on her ankle. Mary bit her lip and waited for Wolfgang to exact his retribution from beyond the grave.

But when she stopped pleading with him, her mind quieted enough for her to notice that the hand at her ankle was warm, the grip gentle. His thumb traced the bump of her ankle bone, and when she opened her eyes, he hadn't advanced on her any further.

"*Meine kleine Maus*," he said, "Am I really so frightening?"

Mary allowed herself to meet his eyes for the first time, and instead of the cold betrayal she'd expected to find, there was only joy, possibly some weariness. But his blue eyes shone with delight.

"Wolf?" Her voice came out in such a high-pitched squeak that she might as well have been a mouse.

"I'm here, my love," he said, and moved her foot so he could sit on the edge of the bed, her foot coming to rest in his lap.

Mary found herself shaking her head in disbelief. "But you're dead."

Wolf's brows dropped, and he pursed his cracked lips, even as he continued to run reverential fingers over her foot. "Is that what they told you?"

"It's what everyone said when you hadn't come home by winter."

"You waited for me?"

"I would still be there if I hadn't lost the baby."

His grip on her foot tightened, not painful, but as if his whole body had stiffened in shock. "You were . . ."

Mary nodded. "I realized just after you left." Tears fell from her eyes again as she remembered those days. The excitement of finally carrying Wolfgang's child, the anticipation of telling him when he returned home. Then the disappointment when he wasn't there on time, then the worry as every new day ended without his return. Her denial that he was gone, even when everyone told her he wasn't coming back. Then the day the bleeding had come and hadn't stopped, and Mary had wondered if she should just let herself bleed to death and let it all be over. "I... I..."

She couldn't force the words out in any language. About how much she had missed him. How losing their child had devastated her. How, until Lettie had befriended her, she'd nearly given up on everything. All she had were tears.

But then Wolf was lifting her into his arms and settling them against the bed's headboard as he cradled her.

He smelled horrible. Like he hadn't bathed in weeks, but he also smelled like dust and horse and sun. She could feel his heartbeat under her cheek, see his pulse in his throat.

"I can't believe you're alive," Mary said once she'd mastered her tears enough to speak.

He kissed the top of her head. "There were days I thought I would not make it back to you. But knowing you were waiting for me kept me going. Did you not get my letters?"

Mary sat up in his arms and shook her head as she removed his hat. His hair was worse than it had been on the first day she'd met him. It was wild and matted. There was a line of dirt across his forehead where the brim of his hat had rested. Mary dabbed at it with the quilt and his skin came away a new color altogether.

"I had no reason to assume you'd lived. You were seen in town and then you disappeared without a trace." She charted his hairline with her fingertips then traveled along his eyebrows and down his nose. She followed the curve of his lip and line of his jaw, even though his beard was worse than his hair. "Where have you been?"

"I was on the road home when a man on a horse who was headed our way for business asked if he could ride with me. Since everyone else had gone back already, I agreed. We'd been on the road for an hour or so when more men rode up on us. I was attacked. I thought they were trying to rob us both, since he was well dressed, but I was the only one who went down. The last thing I remember was the well-dressed man telling me that I would die before he let me steal his happiness. Then he spit in my face. I woke up on a cattle train headed for Chicago."

"You've been in Chicago for a year?" Mary couldn't believe it. Chicago wasn't close, but she couldn't imagine the journey taking more than a month at most. Less time if he were able to find a train.

"I had nothing when I woke. They took my money. My hat. My shoes. I had to find work, shelter, food. I worked in a factory over the winter, saving what I could, but I barely made enough money to pay my room and board, but I wrote you every day so you would know I was on my way back to you. When spring came, I started traveling. A friend sold me his gun for cheap, and I traveled with only what I could carry. When I grew too hungry, I stopped and worked in the towns I could find, depending on the kindness of others to see me home. There were many who did not believe my story."

Mary didn't blame them. If a man approached her on the street with such a tale, she would have directed him to the church for help and then been on her way.

"You must be exhausted," she said, not able to stop touching him. She could not believe he was truly there. She kissed his nose, then his mouth. Wolfgang's hands tightened on her waist, holding her tighter as he sipped from her lips as if she were water. She pulled back when she realized he was likely dehydrated from traveling. "Let me get you a drink. Then I will start a bath for you and find you some food. And I will get you something of uncle's to wear while—"

"Shh, mouse." Wolfgang put a finger to her lips. "There is time for all of that, but first tell me how you wound up with your uncle. How a wedding dress found itself on the back of your door."

Mary confessed everything. Her despair. Her unfaithfulness. How she'd let Frank push her into marriage and then how she'd discovered he wasn't who she thought he was. Mary told Wolf how she and Lettie had conspired to make sure Mary was able to keep the ranch and make sure Frank had no claim to it. How she had been going to go home tomorrow and keep the ranch alive.

"Then I'm glad I took Arthur's fastest horse," Wolfgang said. "If I had come on foot, we would have missed each other."

Arthur was the preacher's son, who had been caring for the cattle during Mary's recovery. "You've been to the ranch?"

"Of course, my little mouse. I looked for you at home first. I was thankful you and Josephine had been corresponding, so I would know where to find you."

"I'm still just thankful you are alive," she said, then ducked her head, "Are you angry with me?"

"How could I be angry with you, my love?" With a caress, he eased her chin up so their eyes met. "I'm not sure I care for your lover, but you had no reason to believe I would ever come back."

Mary threw her arms around his shoulders, vowing she'd never let this man out of her sight again. Holding him felt so right. His arms banded about her like a vice was the most welcoming feeling in the world. Mary was cementing her elation into her memory when she heard Frank's footsteps on the stairs.

They were slow, but purposeful, like he somehow knew what he would find when he reached the top of the stairs.

Indeed, when Frank reached the top of the stairs, he stopped and stared. He wore his best suit, which was rumpled, and dust covered his shoes. His hair was disheveled, his face twisted into an ugly scowl.

"You bitch," he said. "I should have known anyone who would replace her husband with barely a thought could never be faithful. We've been searching the whole neighborhood for you, and you're up here with some wastrel off the street."

Wolfgang had shifted to the side and stood so he was blocking Frank's view of her from the bed. Anger radiated off both men so hot, the attic room might have glowed like a wood stove in winter.

"She's reuniting with her husband, and you," Wolf called him a foul name in German, "are interrupting."

A brief look of shock passed over Frank's face before he schooled it back into his scowl. "Ah, the German. You survived, did you? I was hoping if the blow to the head didn't kill you that getting trampled by cattle might."

Mary gasped and peeked around Wolf's side at the words, but Wolf didn't seem surprised in the slightest. Had Frank been the man who had ridden with Wolf that day? The one behind the ambush?

"Is it me you have a problem with? Germans? Immigrants?"

Frank took another step into the room. "How come you were able to move here? Take free land? Marry the local beauty and prosper when there are people who have been here for generations who are still struggling?"

Mary wanted to yell how Wolfgang had worked hard to buy his homestead after only one year. How he'd worked for a year for a friend of a friend of his family in Kentucky before he'd even been granted his land, and traveled to Kansas with nothing but his banjo and a promise he wasn't sure would be fulfilled.

Wolfgang only growled the way he did when there were predators after the cattle. "I came by what I have honestly."

"Had," Frank corrected, stepping further into the room, pulling his gun from his holster.

Wolf pushed Mary fully behind him, and she clung to his filthy black duster, biting back a sob as she heard Frank's gun cock.

"You're legally dead, Mr. Zimmerman. You have nothing. No land. No assets—" Mary peeked around Wolf's side just in time to see Frank's malevolent grin. "No wife."

"At least I'm not a liar and a thief," Wolf said.

Mary saw Wolfgang's hand twitch at his side, and she knew the gun he'd mentioned earlier must be hidden under his coat. Wolf wouldn't be able to draw it with Frank's gun trained on him.

"Does it count as murder if the victim is already dead, do you think?" Frank asked.

Mary cringed and dug her fingers into Wolf's coat, waiting for the shot, but instead, she heard footsteps in the hallway below. Then Thomas's voice from the bottom of the stairs. "Frank, it's over. Come down and let's put an end to all this."

Mary closed her eyes, tears welling in relief. Finally. Lettie's new beau had come through. She only hoped Thomas had brought a deputy or two, because Frank was not going to back down easily now that he was backed into a corner. He was going to fight like a wild animal.

"You little bitch," Frank said, circling around Wolf to get a glimpse of Mary, shifting the gun's aim to her chest. "You set this up."

Wolf stepped between Mary and the gun again. She was so frightened she could only shake her head. Thomas and Lettie had only been supposed to stop by after the failed wedding to make sure Frank let her go. To make sure he didn't lose his temper with her and do something drastic. She hadn't realized when she'd asked for Lettie's help that Frank was a criminal. She'd never fathomed that he was the reason Wolf had disappeared in the first place.

Mary would never forgive Frank for that. She needed to bathe. To wash the taint of his touch off her body. Even if it had been weeks since they'd been alone together, Mary needed to cleanse herself of him completely.

"You set yourself up, Frank," Thomas's footsteps also started up the stairs. "I only stopped by to check on Mrs. Zimmerman after she missed the wedding."

Thomas emerged into the attic, his gun trained on Frank. The air grew taut, tense, as Frank couldn't decide where to point his gun. He sidestepped again, aimed his gun at Mary, and said, "Why did you miss our wedding, darling?"

Wolfgang lunged for him.

They hit the floor, Frank's gun discharging. The shot flew wide as Mary threw herself to the floor. The two men wrestled for dominance; the gun clasped between them. Thomas yelled for them to stop, but as they rolled toward the stairs, neither man seemed willing to give up. Frank determined to ruin them all; Wolfgang determined to protect her.

Mary screamed and ran for the stairwell as they crested the precipice and fell. She watched them tumble downward as if in slow motion. Wolf's wild hair on top, then Frank's pomaded head beneath, then legs and boots in a tangle.

They hit the bottom with a thud and crack as the gun discharged again. Mary's ears rang with the echo, but she couldn't look away. Wolf lay on top of Frank at the foot of the stairs. For a long minute neither man moved. Then Wolfgang grunted, and shifted. He pushed to his feet, staggered, then fell to his knees. Blood shimmered down the front of his dark coat, and Mary didn't remember descending the stairs, only easing him against the wall, shouting to Lettie to fetch a doctor as she used the wedding dress she snatched on her way down the stairs to stanch the flow of blood from Wolf's shoulder.

It was only when Thomas knelt to examine Frank that Mary realized he was unmoving at her feet. She flinched away after a glance, the unnatural angle of his neck, the faraway look in his eyes, the way, even in death, he seemed too focused on her would haunt her dreams for years.

Instead she concentrated on her husband, murmuring reassurances to him in German as he alternated between grimaces of pain and goofy grins.

He raised one hand to her face, cupping her cheek, and whispering, "*Ich liebe dich, meine Maus*," before losing consciousness.

Chapter Twenty-Five

2017
Matthew

NAOMI HAD PULLED JESS, not just out of the attic, but all the way out the front door before she'd wrapped her arms around her sister. "When I heard the footsteps, I just knew something awful was going to happen, but I couldn't get up the stairs—and I'm so glad you're alright."

Matthew could see Jess's trembling from the porch and went back inside to retrieve her coat. Ana stood by the coat rack, doing up the buttons on her designer wool peacoat. He'd never seen her so pale, so shaken. If it were anybody else, Matthew would feel sorry for them, but he wasn't ready to forgive her yet for the ways she'd hurt Jess.

"How'd you do it?' Ana asked.

Matthew looped Jess's coat over his arm and pulled down the sleeves on his hoodie. "Do what?" he asked, even though he knew exactly what she was asking.

In shock or not, Ana levelled him with an annoyed look, "Make her fall for *you*." The way she looked him up and down with emphasis on the "you," made it clear what Ana meant.

She didn't know how Jess could like anyone that wasn't her, let alone someone who was a different gender from her.

Matthew shook his head. He didn't have time for this. "I didn't do anything," Matthew said as he turned away. "I just gave her space to be herself."

He didn't stick around to hear any more. Matthew needed to be where Jess was, and she was outside freezing to death.

When he made it outside, Jess and Naomi were still strangling each other with relief and affection.

But all it took was Matthew's hand on Jess's arm for her to throw herself at him. "Oh my god, I can't ever go back up there. That was horrible."

He kissed the top of her head, and said, "I know. You don't have to," he said as he rubbed her back, then spread her coat over her shoulders, and she snuggled into his chest as Ana stalked to her car without a word to anyone.

Craig, who Matthew had completely forgotten about, said, "Well, actually. I'm going to need you both upstairs tonight to help with the cleansing."

Both Matthew and Jess turned to face Craig, each without losing hold of the other. "What cleansing?" Matthew asked at the same time Jess said, "Oh, hell no."

Craig held up his hands. "Naomi and I can take care of the two dead people this afternoon. The man on the stairwell will take some effort to move on, but once he's gone, Mary will go on her own."

"Then what do you need us for?" Jess asked.

"We'll need you to cleanse after they're gone and deal with the residual."

"What does that entail?" Matthew asked, afraid of the answer.

"Nothing you weren't going to do tonight anyway. I just need you to do it there." He pointed toward the attic windows.

Matthew and Jess shared a confused look, as Naomi giggled.

"He wants you to get it on in the attic."

"And wash and replace the sheets when you're done," Craig amended.

Jess said, "How?"

Matthew's jaw worked, but he couldn't find words. There were too many questions running through his mind. Would they have an audience? Could they not? How would going back in that room even be sexy? What if Jess didn't want to do it?

"It's simple sex magic," Naomi said with a shrug. "We'll set up the groundwork, salt around the house, cleanse you two with incense, light some white candles and leave you to it. Ooo, what do you think about white roses?" she asked Craig.

He shrugged. "If you can find any."

"But how does that help with the residual haunting?" Matthew finally asked.

Naomi and Craig shared a look that said they clearly thought Jess and Matthew were dense. "The energy from love is so much stronger than the fear and hate that's causing the residual haunting. What we do this afternoon will loosen it up, and what you two do," Naomi rotated her index finger Matthew and Jess's general direction, will push it out and give the room a new energy. A good energy. Happy, new-love energy."

"Sooo, you want us to spend the night up there?" Jess motioned toward the attic windows. "Where that thing just attacked me?"

"He'll be gone," Craig said, his slim shoulders slouching as he nestled his hands into his pockets.

"You're sure?" Matthew asked.

Craig nodded and turned back to the house, staring at the bank of windows where the attic was.

"So, what do we do now?" Jess asked.

Naomi took Jess's arm and steered her toward Matthew's truck. "Go rest, grab something to eat, and meet us back here." She looked at Craig over her shoulder. "When do you think we'll be ready for them?"

He shrugged, "Nine. Maybe ten."

"Perfect," Naomi said. Then she shoved Jess and motioned for Matthew to hurry up and follow. "Go rest. We'll see you back here at nine unless you hear from me otherwise."

Matthew let Jess into his truck. When he hopped into the driver's seat next to her, Jess said. "This is really weird, right? It's not just me?"

"It's definitely not just you." He was still working his mind around it, so much so that he forgot to ask whether she wanted to go to her place for anything and drove them to his house entirely through muscle memory.

Jess must have been equally as distracted, because she followed him inside without comment or complaint. She didn't even offer any sarcastic commentary on his unmade bed, just fell into it next to him and passed out.

Chapter Twenty-Six

Jess

WHEN NAOMI HAD SUGGESTED she rest, it had sounded like the most insane idea Jess had ever heard. She was way too wired from her afternoon cup of coffee coupled with the adrenaline from the ghost attack; Jess thought she'd never sleep again. But by the time they'd arrived at Matthew's house, Jess could barely keep her eyes open. She barely got her shoes off before she fell asleep in Matthew's bed, and when she woke up again, it was dark outside.

She panicked for a second, thinking they were going to be late, but it was just after seven when she checked her phone. They had plenty of time.

Jess rolled over and snuggled into Matthew's side. This was the first time they had been in bed together clothed, and she definitely preferred fewer barriers between his skin and hers. Matthew automatically wrapped an arm around her waist.

"Are we really going to do this?" he asked. His voice was so quiet that if it hadn't been nearly silent in the room, Jess might not have heard him.

"If, and only if, Craig can convince me that bastard is truly gone."

"I'm not sure I understand which parts are residual and which parts aren't."

"Right? Like if we hear footsteps, I'm outta there. This afternoon was too much for me."

Matthew squeezed her in close. "I would be happy to never live through something like that again."

"I'm glad you were there with me though," she said. Jess could feel sleep pulling her back under, and a big part of her just wanted to stay in bed with Matthew forever.

"We've got just enough time to swing by the cafe for dinner. What do you think? Coffee and the pita plate?"

Jess groaned at the idea of coffee. It sounded so warm and comforting. And how could she say no to Matthew when he was luring out of bed with the offer of vegetarian food.

"Okay, but after this is over, one of us has got to learn how to cook."

Matthew only laughed at her, but then he'd fed her olives and cucumbers dipped in hummus, and when they arrived at the inn with their to-go cups full of the last of the day's coffee from the shop, Jess's blood was thrumming with the force of his love.

Naomi met them at the door, waving a burning bundle of fragrant herbs and flowers over both of them as they ascended the porch steps.

"Well?" Jess asked when Naomi didn't say anything.

She held up a finger as she finished waving the herbs over them, and that's when Jess realized she was chanting under her breath. When she was done, she beamed at Jess, then flashed a sly grin at Matthew. "You're golden. Have fun you two; I'm gonna go crash."

"Is Craig still here?" Matthew asked.

"Just left. We did our part. Now it's up to you guys. Don't let us down, now."

Naomi was most of the way down the sidewalk by then. Jess clenched her teeth and looked up at the front door. She could do this. She and her boyfriend were just here to spend some quality time together. Like a weekend getaway. Like the inn was already open, but they had the place all to themselves.

Jess squeezed Matthew's hand hard, then said, "Race you to the bed?" Then took off before she could think twice about sprinting into the dark house. The light was on in the stairwell, and she ran all the way up to the attic, then regretted it as she had to wait at the top of the stairs listening to Matthew's heavy footfalls as he caught up to her.

He wore a grin as he crested the top of the stairs, as if he'd been enjoying the game, but it fell as he took in the room over Jess's shoulder. She'd been concentrating so hard on the footsteps; she hadn't even noticed. But the footsteps had stopped when Matthew had. All Jess heard now was the pounding of her heart in her ears.

Then Matthew said, "Did you see this?"

Behind her, the whole attic apartment was bathed in candlelight. White pillars dotted every surface, each with bright, happy looking flames. Jess's eyes followed a trail of white rose petals to the bed.

"Did we ask the significance of the white?" Matthew asked.

"It's for purification," Jess said. "It helps draw out what's left of the negative energy. I'm sure there's salt hidden all over the place too."

It took a second for Jess to realize that Matthew was staring at her. "What? Naomi has been into this stuff since she was, like, a baby. She used to make me cast spells with her."

Matthew reached for her then. "It's kind of romantic, don't you think?"

"Yeah, it is." She allowed him to nestle her into his chest, as they both got lost watching the multitude of flickering flames. At some point they started swaying to some unheard rhythm. It was silly, but nice. Something Jess had seen her parents do a million times in the kitchen growing up.

"We can't do this for guests though," she said. "It's totally a fire hazard."

"Oh, absolutely," Matthew agreed.

He brushed her straight hair out of her face and cupped her cheeks with both hands. "I think this might be the strangest thing I've ever done."

"You haven't done anything yet."

A breath of a laugh escaped his lips. "Is that a challenge?"

"I could make it one. I did win the race."

Matthew ducked down and captured her lower lip between his teeth. "False. You haven't made it to the bed yet, love." But then he was kissing her, nipping at her lips as he backed her toward the bed.

He stopped just short, first unbuttoning her coat, then dropping it and his hoodie to the floor. He unraveled her scarf, then pulled off first one boot then the other before removing his own shoes.

"I really like your feet," she said.

"My feet?" He pulled his shirt off as if to say *I have muscles and you're attracted to my feet?*

Jess traced a fingernail through his sprinkling of chest hair and down his abdomen toward his belt. "Yeah, there's something oddly intimate about seeing someone barefoot. I like getting to see your feet."

"I always seem to get distracted before I get to your feet," Matthew said as his hands inched her sweater up and up, exposing the black lace bra that barely held her boobs in. She'd been slowly upping her lingerie game since their first night together. Matthew's curse and subsequent disposal of her sweater was exactly the reaction she'd been hoping for.

"I hope it doesn't sound cliche when I say I love your breasts." His hands went straight for the lace cups and squeezed. "I mean, I know it's not as unique as having a foot fetish, but—"

He jumped away with a yowl when Jess pinched his side.

"It's not a fetish," she said.

"Jeez, okay." Matthew took her jaw in his hand and raised her chin at the same time he ducked down to kiss her. "It's not a fetish, just an appreciation of shared intimacy. I get it."

"Thank you," Jess said, then sucked his lower lip into her mouth hard enough to make him growl, and she knew this was going to be good.

CURTAINS. JESS WAS going to need to talk to Nell about getting curtains for the window by the bed, because the winter sun woke her too damn early. She wasn't exactly sure what time she and Matthew had gone to sleep, but they might have doubled-up on their part of the cleansing, just in case.

Jess sighed as she remembered joking about not being sure the first time had taken, even while she'd already been riding him. The one and only reason had been because she couldn't get enough of him, cleansing be damned, this man was hers.

Even as she'd watched him blow out all the candles before climbing in bed with her, limbs heavy with boneless exhaustion, she looked forward to the next time they came together.

Jess tried to roll away from the window and go back to sleep, but her bladder called. She pulled on her jeans and wrapped herself in Matthew's hoodie, partially because it was freezing outside the bed, and partially because of the whole no-curtains thing. She used the bathroom, and since there were no dishes in the little kitchen yet, Jess rinsed out her coffee cup from the night before and drank tap water from that.

She walked the perimeter of the apartment as quietly as she could given the creaky floors. She could feel the difference in the room. It was calm, serene, peaceful, just like it should be on a cold winter morning. It was idyllic, with even a fresh dusting of snow on the ground outside. It had been a surprisingly dry winter until now, and Jess felt like this snow was just for them. A celebration for a whole night without footsteps.

When Jess made it back to the bed, it was to find Matthew propped on an elbow, watching her. She offered him a drink of water, and he took it, draining what was left in one gulp. He handed back the empty cup and said, "You're wearing too many clothes."

Jess set the cup on the bedside table and allowed Matthew to pull her onto him so she was straddling his thighs. "This room has zero curtains and there are people outside shoveling their driveways."

"So, prudent this morning." He inched the zipper on the hoodie down a salacious few inches and parted the fabric to reveal just enough of her breasts to be indecent without exposing her. "You do look good in my hoodie, though."

She looked down to where his fingers traced the skin over her sternum. The hoodie probably used to be brown, but it was so faded it was more of an ugly khaki color. It looked fantastic on him, but Jess would never wear it outside of this bedroom.

"I think it worked," she said. "I think your Mama Zim is finally at rest with her husband."

Matthew's hands traced down her arms until he intwined the fingers on both hands with hers. "In all the excitement yesterday, I didn't get a chance to tell you that I heard back from my aunt about Wolfgang."

"Oooo, yeah. Tell me about the miraculous disappearing man," Jess said, scooting herself higher up Matthew's thighs, her eyes roving over the exposed muscles on his chest. He was beautiful.

"Apparently there's a whole family legend that her gramps used to tell, but nobody thought it was real. It went that Wolfgang was kidnapped during a cattle drive because he and Mary apparently owned a ton of land, and some smarmy city guy didn't like an immigrant having so much, so he schemed to off Wolfgang, marry Mary, then sell the land at a profit and take the money. Only Wolfgang escaped before any of that could happen and killed the other guy."

"And that happened in this house?" Jess asked.

Matthew shrugged. "I guess so."

"I wonder what the connection was."

Matthew pulled her down on top of him. "Well, we have the article about Wolfgang's disappearance. Now that we know what we're looking for, I bet it wouldn't take that much digging to find out."

"I am definitely calling my librarian today."

Jess was pretty sure Matthew didn't hear what she'd just said. His eyes were glued to her boobs, which were pretty much spilling out of his hoodie onto his chest.

"What time is it? And more importantly, do we have enough time before the crew shows up?" he asked, his voice already tight with desire.

Jess glanced up to the window above them, trying to guess the time by the sun. "I don't know. Maybe thirty minutes?"

"That's enough time, yeah?"

Jess answered him with a kiss.

When Jess buttoned her coat half an hour later, her phone vibrated in the pocket. It was a text from her sister telling her not to forget to wash the sheets, but Matthew was already stripping the bed.

Epilogue One

WOLFGANG DIDN'T GO on the cattle drive this year; he'd sent the preacher's son in his stead. He'd become an apprentice of sorts and had helped them tremendously when they'd returned from the city. The gunshot wound in Wolf's shoulder had taken months to heal properly, even though, or perhaps because, he'd insisted he was fine to get back to work after a week.

Mary was tempted to ask Wolf never to leave for the cattle drive again, but she knew she wouldn't always have the excuse she had this year. Maybe she would if she was lucky. And when he was away, Mary would read the letters they'd recovered from Frank's office. He'd been intercepting her mail. He'd known Wolfgang was alive the entire time, and Mary would never forgive him for that. But at least she had both her husband and his letters, and she was confident that when he left for the cattle drive next year, Wolfgang would fly back to her side.

For now, Mary would enjoy the warm weather while they still had it, sitting in the rocker on the porch while Wolfgang picked a quiet song on his banjo and Mary nursed their two-week old son. Matthew. Their miracle boy that cemented this life of theirs together at last.

As Mary met Wolf's fond gaze, she knew this was exactly where she wanted to be, and she would never stop being thankful that this was her life.

Epilogue Two

2018
Matthew
One Year Later

DESPITE IT BEING A huge part of Jess's life, Matthew hadn't been back to the Wolf and Mary Inn since opening day. They'd celebrated with an open house and a cocktail hour on the main floor to welcome the new manager and the first set of guests. Between his book tour and helping Dana keep Zimmerman-Dartmouth running, Matthew hadn't had time to visit. He'd forgotten there were pictures of his ancestors everywhere.

To anyone who didn't know the story, they just looked like tasteful antique black and white photographs, but a photo of Wolfgang sitting astride a horse and the photograph of Mary in her wedding dress were framed behind the front desk.

The manager emerged from the office just as Matthew set his overnight bag on the floor. It was impossible to know if he'd beaten Jess there or not. She usually parked in the back now that the inn was open.

"Mr. Zimmerman," the woman said with a smile. She was about his age, pretty, and Jess raved about how wonderful she was.

Matthew held out his hand. "Please, it's just Matthew."

"Kat," she said, though Matthew knew that, of course. "Jess isn't here yet, but she told me to go ahead and show you on up to the suite—though I suppose you know the way."

He'd opened his mouth to reply when Kat said, "I'm sorry. I told myself I was going to be cool when you came in, and I'm sure you get this all the time, but I just loved your book, and I was wondering if you wouldn't mind signing my copy?"

She was wrong. Matthew hardly ever got asked this question outside of signings. His book was selling well, but it wasn't like people recognized him on the street or anything.

"Of course," he said. "I'd be happy to."

Kat turned bright red and pulled his book out from behind the counter. Matthew grabbed a pen from the mug next to the computer and was just handing the book back to Kat when Jess burst through the front door, stomping snow off her boots.

"Oh good, you got your book signed. I told you he'd do it."

"Thank you so much," Kat said to Matthew, ignoring her boss.

"I'll bring you an advanced copy of the newest one. It's even better," Jess said. "Now, how are the kids doing? Last time I was here, they were giving you a hard time."

Kat's sad smile said enough. From what he knew from Jess, Kat had just separated from her husband when she took the job at the Inn, and the divorce had finalized sometime in the last few months. Matthew hadn't asked about the details, but he had the impression the whole thing had been messy.

"They're with their dad this week, so I'm sure they're happy. And Asher and Oscar are even more inseparable these days, so it's fun for them to be over there."

"Oscar is a lot of fun, but you know they totally miss you when they're gone, right? I've seen them right after they come back; they can't wait to tell you everything. That's a good thing."

Kat nodded, and Matthew couldn't tell if she was on the verge of tears because of the toll her divorce had taken on her or because Jess's words had pleased her. Matthew's heart went out to the woman, but he was here for a specific reason, and he was anxious to get to it.

Even so, he couldn't keep himself from asking, "Who is Oscar?" on their way up the stairs a minute later.

"You remember Naomi's old roommate, Rachel?"

"Vaguely. Though I think we only met the once."

"Right. Well, Oscar is her kid. He's the same age as Kat's son Asher, and Kat's ex-husband is with Rachel now, so . . ."

"Ah. Too much drama for me."

Jess giggled as they pushed into the suite formerly known as the haunted attic. "Tell me about it. Makes me even more thankful for the quiet little life I have with you."

"Thanks?"

Jess swatted him on his butt as he set their bags on the bed. "It was a compliment, you doof."

"Sure sounded like," he said, but caught her up in his arms anyway. She shrieked with laughter as he pretended to gnaw on her neck in the precise place he'd learned she was ticklish.

He stopped when Jess smacked his shoulder and captured her lips in a kiss. "Happy anniversary," he whispered.

It had been one year since the day they'd first slept together. They'd decided that was their anniversary rather than the day before, just so they'd have an extra day to recover from New Year's.

"I can't believe I've put up with you for a whole year," Jess said, even as she fisted her fingers into his hair.

"Oh, you put up with me, did you?"

She laughed in delight when Matthew patted her bottom, and she hopped up so her legs wrapped around his waist, so he could dump her back onto the bed. "Obviously," she managed to force out between giggles and kisses. "Your author ego has really been out of control lately."

Matthew grinned. He only had an author ego because of her. She'd managed to push his book from relatively obscure new release to acclaimed first novel. His publisher had even spaced out his releases in order to build more hype. But that meant Jess had him posting on social media and doing podcast interviews, even a few television ones. He still felt ridiculous every time, but she was pushing him, slowly but surely, out of his shell. And he was building her a house.

She didn't know that yet. But he was going to tell her tonight. Let her pick out where she wanted it, what she wanted it to look like, and then they would build it together. Maybe they'd have a couple kids. Maybe they wouldn't. They'd already decided not to get married. Her mom and Dana were conspiring to throw them a "Forever Person" party over the summer, and Jess had decided to let them.

Matthew would basically give her whatever she wanted. She was so bright and so caring, he couldn't bring himself to do anything that would dim her luster.

Matthew pulled back to yank her ridiculous boots from her feet, but she clamped her legs around his hips and pulled down by the collar of his shirt. "You know I love you, right?"

"Sweetheart, I've never had any doubt," he said, and kissed her until she panted for him.

THANK YOU FOR READING!

I hope you enjoyed reading *Haunted Attraction*. This book has been ruminating in my brain since October 2016 (hence the timeline). It started out as a kernel of a story with two timelines, ghosts, and a love story. When I started writing it during Nanowrimo in November of 2016, that was all I had. I didn't know Matthew was going to be a lanky teddy bear though I had a good idea that Jess was going to be prickly, because let's face it most of my heroines are. But I didn't get to finish the book that November. (It's the only Nanowrimo I've "lost" since 2014.) I had a three-month-old baby, and I was working two jobs. Something had to give. But I never gave up on wanting to make this story a reality. I loved it too much. So this past summer after I'd finished up The Incident Series, and before I went back to my day job, I decided to go for it. And I'm so glad I did. This book turned out to be everything I ever wanted it to be, which, if you are any kind of artist, you know is a difficult, almost impossible task, but Haunted Attraction somehow managed to reach that vision. Special thanks to E and C for being the best beta readers ever. Truly, I'd be lost without you.

And, if you're a fan of Jess's sister, Naomi, you're in luck. She'll be in the upcoming Lightning Crashes Duet, which may or may not have something to do with the characters mentioned in the epilogue.

Want to Connect with Me?

I am @marlaholtauthor[1] on Instagram. I'd love to see your bookstagram posts or just chat about the book.

I can't wait to meet you!

Finally, leaving reviews is one of the best ways you can support the Indie Authors you love. I'd be forever in your debt if you took the time to review *Haunted Attraction*

---

1. http://instagram.com/marlaholtauthor

Also By Marla Holt

When Abe Met Lane: The Prequel Novella to The Other Lane[1]
The Other Lane: A Modern Fairy Tale[2]
The Try Again Series:
Ethan & Juliet: An Opposites Attract Second Chance Romance[3]
Sparkle & Shine: A Second Chance Romance[4]
Read & Wright: A Second Chance Romance[5]
The Incident Series:
Love, Van B: And Incident Series Novella[6]
The Van Birch Incident: A Forbidden Rock Star Romance[7]
The Deception Incident: A Secret Baby Romance[8]
The Betrayal Incident: An Age Gap Romance[9]

---

1. https://amzn.to/3kaKU9a

2. https://amzn.to/2Pox6d1

3. https://amzn.to/2Xpsnfp

4. https://amzn.to/2Dx2weA

5. https://amzn.to/33rv5Fl

6. https://amzn.to/31gJstq

7. https://amzn.to/2XrldHR

8. https://amzn.to/33ragd1

9. https://amzn.to/2GhRHyD

www.ingramcontent.com/pod-product-compliance
Lightning Source LLC
Chambersburg PA
CBHW050714180626
46814CB00002B/425